Literature In...

# Reading *Catch-22*

Paul McDonald

𝓗𝓔𝓑 ☼ Humanities-Ebooks, LLP

© Paul McDonald, 2012

The Author has asserted his right to be identified as the author of this Work in accordance with the Copyright, Designs and Patents Act 1988.

First published by *Humanities-Ebooks, LLP,*
Tirril Hall, Tirril, Penrith CA10 2JE

Cover image © Sean Gladwell - Fotolia.com

This title is available as a Pdf ebook from http://www.humanities-ebooks.co.uk and to libraries from EBSCO and MyiLibrary.

ISBN 978-1-84760-200-8 Pdf Ebook
ISBN 978-1-84760-201-5 Kindle Ebook
ISBN 978-1-4716-221541-2 Paperback

# Contents

## 1. Introduction — 7

## 2. A Biography of Joseph Heller — 9
*2.1. Early Life* — *9*
*2.2. Heller as a Soldier* — *10*
*2.3. Heller after the War* — *11*
*2.4. Finding a Voice* — *12*
*2.5. The Genesis of Catch 22* — *14*
*2.6. Catch-22 is Published* — *16*
*2.7. The Cultural Moment of Catch-22* — *17*
*2.8 Heller after Catch-22* — *19*

## 3. Literary strategies — 23
*3.1. Humour in Catch-22* — *23*
*3.2. The Structure and Realism in Catch-22* — *25*
*3.3. Influences* — *28*

## 4. *Catch-22* - Sequential Development and Analysis — 33
*4.1. Chapters One to Six* — *33*
*4.2. Chapters Seven to Thirteen* — *37*
*4.3. Chapters Fourteen to Twenty* — *39*
*4.4. Chapters Twenty One to Twenty Seven* — *44*
*4.5. Chapters Twenty Eight to Thirty Five* — *49*
*4.6. Chapters Thirty Six to Forty Two* — *53*

## 5. Interpreting *Catch-22* — 59
*5.1. Yossarian as Individualist Hero* — *59*
*5.2. Yossarian and Contemporary America* — *62*
*5.3. Yossarian as Mythic Hero* — *64*

| | |
|---|---|
| *5.4. Yossarian as Postmodern Hero.* | *67* |
| *5.5. Yossarian as the Hero of a Bad Novel* | *70* |
| *5.6. Yossarian as an Old Man: Closing Time* | *73* |
| **6. Bibliography** | **79** |
| *6.1. Other Relevant Books by Heller* | *79* |
| *6.2. Catch-22 Film* | *79* |
| *6.3. Books about Heller* | *80* |
| *6.4. Books on Modern American Writing* | *81* |
| *6.5. Online Material* | *81* |
| **A Note on the Author** | **83** |

# 1. Introduction

*Catch-22* is one of the most successful books in history, selling over ten million copies. Currently its average annual sales are roughly 85,000. It is considered to be a key contribution to American letters, and continues to attract a huge amount of critical attention from scholars. Few books can boast this level of significance, and fewer still can claim to have invented a term that is recognisable across the English speaking world. Despite its staggering success, *Catch-22* is a challenging, occasionally bewildering novel that demands close attention. This guide is designed to help readers navigate their way through the book, understand something of its context, and learn about some of the ways in which it has been interpreted in the half-century since its publication.

## 2. A Biography of Joseph Heller

### 2.1. Early Life

The author of *Catch-22* was born in Coney Island, New York on 1 May 1923 to Russian-Jewish parents, Lena and Isaac Heller. Isaac died when Heller was 4, which meant that he, and his two older half-siblings, Sylvia and Lee, grew up in relative poverty. Despite this set back, his childhood seems to have been a happy one. Coney Island in the 20s and 30s was quite an exciting place for a young boy, with its fairground attractions, and the ocean close at hand. It seems to have been an ideal environment for Heller to develop his sense of fun, and his fondness for bizarre humour. He was certainly something of a daredevil, attracted to dangerous games such as swimming far out into the Atlantic, a feat at which he risked his life on several occasions. He also had a vivid imagination, sensing from an early age that he might have the makings of a writer. He was strongly drawn to stories, and the first to have a major impact on him was a prose translation of Homer's *Iliad*, which he read over and over when he was young. Many of his own early tales are influenced by this, as well as by the very short twist-in the-tale stories found in places like *Collier's* magazine, copies of which were supplied to him by his older brother and sister. As an adolescent he began reading Damon Runyon, and humourists such as P.G. Wodehouse and Robert Benchley, who appealed to the young man's developing fondness for comedy and satire. He admits in his memoir, *Now and Then* (1998), that his early attempts at writing were 'spectacularly immature and inept,'[1] but he soon felt confident enough to begin submitting to journals. Aged 16 he submitted his first piece for publication, a

---

[1] Joseph Heller. *Now and Then: A Memoir from Coney Island to Here*. (London: Simon & Schuster, 1998) 42

war story inspired by Russia's invasion of Finland and focusing on a heroic soldier defending his post against the Russian army. It was rejected from several magazines, but thankfully this didn't undermine Heller's enthusiasm for writing.

## 2.2. Heller as a Soldier

Heller had several jobs after graduating from Abraham Lincoln High School in 1941, and he continued to write short stories. With WWII raging in Europe, however, it soon became clear to him that this would have a bearing on his future, and he eventually enlisted in the Army Air Corps on 19 October, 1942. The thrill of adventure that inspired Heller to play his dangerous swimming games seems to feature in his thinking here too; in one interview he states that:

> The day I enlisted was like going off to watch a baseball game [...] I went out with great good sprits, went with a few friends [...] Had no idea what we were doing except that what we were going to do was more exciting, more romantic, more adventurous than what we were doing at home.[1]

Clearly he sees joining the military more as an opportunity than an obligation, although given that the draft age had recently been lowered to 19 years, he would not ultimately have had much choice in the matter.

Heller trained as a B25-Bombadier, which is Yossarian's role in *Catch-22*. A bombardier is the person whose job it is to guide the bomber to the target and release the bombs at the correct time in order to achieve maximum impact. In 1944 he was sent to Corsica to fly with 488th Bombardment Squadron, 12th Air Force. He flew a total of 60 missions, and he claims that he enjoyed his experience of the war for the most part. Undoubtedly he felt that it was a justified conflict, as most Americans did following the Japanese attack on Pearl Harbour in 1941; however, he was no stranger to some of the fears that torment Yossarian in the novel. In *Now and Then* he tells of one harrowing experience over Avignon when his squadron encoun-

---

1 Quoted in Tracy Daugherty. *Just One Catch: A Biography of Joseph Heller.* (New York: St. Martin's Press, 2011) 66

tered heavy flak. The co-pilot of his plane climbed sharply away, but fearing they were about to stall he put them into a steep dive. The experience is almost identical to Yossarian's mission in *Catch-22* when Snowden is killed. After Heller's plane was brought under control he made his way to the rear and encountered a wounded man, much as Yossarian finds Snowden in the novel. On that occasion the man didn't die, but Heller drew on his experience of another mission when someone *was* fatally wounded in order to depict the graphic and horrifying details of Snowden's demise in Yossarian's arms. So Heller had some harrowing wartime exploits that reflect Yossarian's, and, like Yossarian, he admits to being afraid—he was scared every time he went up in a plane after the incident over Avignon, and even following the war it was many years before Heller could summon the courage to travel by air. When he was finally able to fly again he was invariably terrified by the prospect, so much so that, according to his daughter, he would always travel in a separate plane from his wife so that, in the event of a crash, there would be someone left to look after the children![1] Yossarian's terror, the source of both comedy and unease in the novel, is grounded at least partly in Heller's own sense of dread following his traumatic occupation as a bombardier.

So Heller draws on the facts of his own life in *Catch-22*. While he changes the location of the airbase from Corsica to Pianosa, some of the incidents—like the Avignon mission—are grounded in reality, and many of the characters are based on real people, including Hungry Joe, Major —— de Coverley, and Orr. However, as we'll see, it is a mistake to think of *Catch-22* as a novel which seeks to accurately depict, or even comment on WWII. Most critics see it as reflecting the period in American culture after the war, and certainly Heller himself thought object of his satire was contemporary rather than historical.

## 2.3. Heller after the War

Heller returned to America something of a glamorous hero; he had been awarded a medal following his actions over Avignon, and he

---

1 See Erica Heller, *Yossarian Slept Here: When Joseph Heller was Dad and Life was a Catch*-22 (London: Vintage, 2011) 49–50

was quite a striking figure: good-looking and quick-witted. It wasn't long before he met, fell in love with and married a young woman, Shirley, the daughter of a respectable Jewish family. He decided to study English at the University of Southern California using money from the G.I. Bill to finance his course—this was a bill that provided funding and loans to help returning veterans reestablish themselves in society after service. Throughout his life Heller would speak of his debt to this provision, without which it would have been impossible for him to gain a University education. Before the war very few people with backgrounds such as Heller's made it to University, and the fact that the G.I. Bill facilitated this privilege for many working class people had a significant social and cultural impact in the U.S. In Heller's case it gave him time and space to develop his talent for writing, and exposed him to a variety of authors and thinkers he might not otherwise have encountered, both at the University of Southern California, and later at the universities of New York and Columbia. He received an MA from the latter, before winning a Fulbright scholarship to Oxford University in 1950.

**2.4. Finding a Voice**

Heller had not stopped writing fiction whilst overseas, and soon after his return to the States in 1945 he published his first story in a periodical called *Story*. Titled, 'I Don't Love You Any More,' it is the tale of a young war veteran who returns home to find that he no longer cares for his wife. Though the story helped confirm Heller's belief in his own talent, it has nothing of his distinctive voice. It is extremely derivative of the fiction he had been reading in the early 1940s, and the kind of literary models he held in esteem, particularly Ernest Hemingway, William Saroyan, and John O'Hara. These were regarded as the foremost authors of the time, and his first story feels like an exercise in emulation, with nothing of Heller's personality present in the writing. As his reading broadened, however, so did the influences on his style: he developed a fondness for the acerbic American humorist H.L.Mencken, and he also discovered Jerome Weidman, a writer whose colloquial language captures the spirit of New York Jewish people. This humorous and less formal writing seems to have had an impact, and the freer prose style in his 1948 short story, 'Castle of Snow,' is something of a breakthrough, the first indication that he was beginning to move away from imitation toward a voice that was more his own.

Arguably the first major American novel about WWII is Norman Mailer's *The Naked and the Dead*, published in 1948. This is based on Mailer's experiences during the Philippines Campaign, and it was extremely successful both critically and commercially. It employs what might be called a realist–naturalist style. The terms realism and naturalism in literature refer to writing that attempts to represent the world as accurately and objectively as possible, without contrivance or romantic distortion. Realism emerged in Europe in the nineteenth century and was embraced by American writers as the style best suited to addressing the social consequences of industrial expansion after the Civil War (1861–1865). Novelists like William Dean Howells (1837–1920), Frank Norris (1870–1902) and Theodore Dreiser (1871–1945) are associated with the form, along with numerous others. The term naturalism applies to harsh, uncompromising examples of realism where characters' lives are seen to be conditioned by social forces. Realism–naturalism continued to be influential in the twentieth century, particularly during the Depression among writers like John Steinbeck (1902–1968) and James T. Farrell (1904–1979). However, though perfectly suited to Mailer's purpose in the *Naked and the Dead*, this approach had come to feel a little outdated by the mid-twentieth century. This is something that Heller was conscious of and, as Tracy Daugherty says, 'The more he read—the greater variety of literature he was exposed to—the more he recognized that contemporary American writing, hobbled by outmoded conventions, was unable to document that nation's new realities' (Daugherty, *Just One Catch*, 126). In other words he began to feel that American writing was passé and inadequate, and that included his own. He was becoming increasingly impressed with writing that was less traditional-realist, and more experimental in style: writers such as Louis-Ferdinand Céline, William Faulkner, Franz Kafka, Vladimir Nabokov, Evelyn Waugh and Nathaniel West, seemed to have more potential to capture the contemporary experience. He was inspired by the way they use dark humour, surrealism and absurdity, and particularly by the way they were able to find humour in tragedy. This kind of writing appeared more relevant to the times for Heller partly because American culture was changing quickly. For one thing, television had become enormously important, providing a platform for a variety of popular art forms, particularly Jewish American humour. The 1950s saw the emergence of key comics like Milton Berle, Jack Benny and Sid Caesar, among many others. Jewish humour became central to American culture throughout the decade that Heller was searching for his voice as a writer. Humour was also a significant part of Heller's job in the 1950s. After a period as a university lecturer, he took employment in advertising, becoming a copywriter with *Time* magazine in 1955, and later with *Look* magazine, and *McCall's*. Here he learned something about the rhetorical importance of humour, an appreciation of the persuasive power of wit. So these are some of the factors that influence Heller's developing authorial voice; of specific importance is his increasing appreciation of the value of comedy, both in terms of its cultural significance, and its artistic validity and potential.

## 2.5. The Genesis of Catch 22

There are several different accounts of how the theme and tone of *Catch-22* began to develop in Heller's imagination, all of which are related in Tracy Daugherty's biography. He once claimed that he was inspired by conversations he had with two war veterans, one of whom would speak humorously about of his war experiences, while the other was unable to see the relevance of humour to the misery of conflict:

> I tried to explain the first one's point of view to the second. He recognised that traditionally there had been lots of graveyard humour, but he could not reconcile it with what he had seen of war (Daugherty, *Just One Catch*, 175).

This difference of opinion set Heller thinking about the best strategy for his subject matter, and what potential there might be in the relationship between comedy and despair. Elsewhere Heller expresses a debt to Jaroslav Hašek's book, *The Good Soldier Schweik* (1930), which is a black comedy set in Austria-Hungary during WWI. This war novel has an unfortunate hero at the centre of the plot and, like *Catch-22*, is full of absurdist humour intended to expose the futility of war. In many interviews Heller also claimed that the novel was really born when the first line came to him: 'It was love at first sight. The first time he saw the chaplain, Someone fell madly in love with him' (Daugherty, *Just One Catch*, 176). He didn't initially have a name for the 'Someone,' of course, but this line apparently provided a catalyst for the book, and throughout his career Heller maintained that all his novels would take shape only after he had formulated an effective opening line.

Enthused by the potential of his first line, Heller wrote a short story called 'Catch-18,' which would eventually become the opening chapter of the novel. He submitted it to an agent, Candida Donadio, who was impressed. Not everyone was, and the story was rejected numerous times on the grounds that the comedy seemed silly, and at odds with the subject of war. Donadio persisted and eventually it was accepted by *New World Writing*, where it was published in 1955. Heller received a cheque for $25. The story appeared alongside a piece called 'Jazz of the Beat Generation,' which is a section from what would become another ground-breaking American novel, Jack Kerouac's *On the Road* (1957).

The subsequent development of the complete novel was slow. Heller constructed it using index cards on which he would write details of characters, scenes, and missions. After working these up into draft chapters he would show them to Donadio, and to various friends whose opinions he trusted. The feedback was not always positive, as some felt that the writing appeared fragmentary and unintelligible, devoid of obvious commercial appeal. People did tend to agree that it was funny, however, and he received enough positive feedback to continue the project. Eventually Simon and Schuster decided to take the novel, and Heller worked with their editor, Robert Gottlieb, who helped him shape his huge original manuscript into a publishable form. As his daughter says, 'he wrote it for nine years, which turned out to be an average gestation period for his books' (Erica Heller, *Yossarian Slept Here*, 32)

## 2.6. Catch-22 is Published

Because the book is based partly on Heller's own life there was concern that the publisher might be subject to litigation if people who served with him recognised or misread characters as versions of themselves. While Heller didn't feel the relationship between fact and fiction was strong enough to warrant making major changes, he did accept the need to alter the location of the island airbase from Corsica to Pianosa. The latter is a real island in the Mediterranean, but not large enough to accommodate an airbase the size of the one in the book. He also had to change the title. Throughout the project the working title had been *Catch-18*, following the initial story, but at the last minute they had to find another because Leon Uris—a popular novelist at the time—was due to publish a book called *Mila 18*, and it was felt there would be a confusing clash. Most would probably agree that 22 makes for a much better title; the repetition in the number has a pleasing sound, and is appropriate for a story based around recurrences, of scenes that are revisited time and again, characters who experience *déjà vu*, or who see everything twice, missions that will seemingly never end, and so on.

*Catch-22* was first published on 10 October, 1961 with an initial printing of 4000 copies. It sold sluggishly at first, and not all of the reviews were favourable. As Heller himself says:

> The novel was not the instant success many people assume it was, not at all on the scale of such immediate national acclaim as greeted the first novels of Normal Mailer, James Jones, and others. It was not a best-seller and it won no prizes. There were reviews that were good, a good many that were mixed, and there were reviews that were bad, very bad, almost venomously spiteful (Heller, *Now and Then*, 222).

By contrast, when the novel was published in the UK a few months later, it was an almost instant hit—it received very good reviews and moved quickly up the best-seller lists. This in turn boosted its popularity in the U.S. and there was a surge in sales, particularly when the paperback edition was published by Dell. Surprisingly, however, Heller claims not to have made much money from the book at first, paperback copies only earning him a meagre 'three or four cents a copy.' It was not until he managed to sell the film rights a year after the initial publication that he risked relinquishing his job at *McCall's* magazine (Heller, *Now and Then*, 223).

## 2.7. The Cultural Moment of Catch-22

Through the early to mid-60s the book became a publishing phenomenon, and Joseph Heller enjoyed the status of literary celebrity, in demand for interviews in newspapers, and on radio and TV. Daugherty notes that something of a *Catch-22* craze developed in the States: stickers bearing the words 'YOSSARIAN LIVES' appeared on buildings, and a fashion for army jackets bearing Yossarian name-tags took hold among students. The phrase, 'Catch-22', itself also quickly took hold in everyday discourse as one denoting illogical, no-win situations, particularly in relation to bureaucratic institutions (see Daugherty, *Just One Catch*, 238-240).

All of this attests to the success of the novel, of course, but is also illustrates that it was part of a broader socio-cultural phenomenon, reflecting the public mood in 1960s America. Its publication came at the start of a decade that began optimistically, with the election of John F. Kennedy—a young, Democratic president who seemed to offer a new way forward—but which later witnessed increasing cynicism, particularly among young people. As the decade developed Americans suffered much that would undermine the initial optimism: the assassinations of JFK, of his brother Robert, and of Martin Luther King; at the same time there were battles for civil rights which included rioting in many American cities, and, of particular significance for the success of *Catch-22*, the Vietnam War. Cynicism toward the establishment came in the form counterculture movements such as the Hippies, many of whom were of the opinion that the powers-that-be in America were duplicitous and inept, as Malcolm Bradbury and Daniel Snowman have written:

> By the end of 1968, it seemed to many that there were two distinct American societies existing side by side—an 'official' America [...] and a counterculture of hippies, yippies, political activists, angry blacks, alienated youngsters, disenchanted parents.[1]

It is easy to see why a novel like *Catch-22* would appeal to those who were suspicious of the 'official' version of America, and who had begun to question the competence of those who were supposed to be in control. In Heller's novel the official version of the facts—for instance the 'death' of Doc Daneeka—is often a blatant misrepresentation of reality; similarly, the people responsible for managing the war, like those running the country in the 1960s, have their own interests at heart.

For many people the novel also captured the peculiar, often bizarre-seeming nature of post-war American life. The novelist Philip Roth, in a 1961 article 'Writing American Fiction,' for instance, discusses the difficulty modern American novelists seemed to be having in capturing the 'unreality' of America in a credible way. According to Roth, American reality had become so strange that fiction writers struggled to do it justice—it was outstripping their imaginative capacity.[2] Arguably this phenomenon was compounded by new cultural forms such as television, which fed the public's desire for sensationalism and facile entertainment. As the critic Tony Hilfer says, 'The media culture seems to have effectively reduced the most dramatic stories we tell ourselves from high tragedy to demented farce.' Some writers responded by embracing 'demented farce,' and 'readers found their own experience mirrored in the writer's vision.'[3] In many ways *Catch 22* offers such a vision; certainly many feel that it captures this sense of unreality. It constructs a world in which the absurd appears normal, and the only option seems to be to adapt to it.

Numerous critics have observed shifts in attitude and style associated with American fiction in the 1960s, and this includes the arrival of several writers whose work, like Heller's, used black humour to sati-

---

1  Daniel Snowman and Malcolm Bradbury, 'The Sixties and Seventies,' in Malcolm Bradbury and Howard Temperley, eds., *Introduction to American Studies* 2nd edition (Harlow: Longman, 1989, 323–361) 342.
2  Philip Roth 'Writing American Fiction,' *Commentary*, March 1961.
3  Tony Hilfer. *American Fiction Since 1940* (Harlow: Longman, 1992) 115.

rize some of America's cherished institutions. Such material seems to tap in to the cynicism and sense of the absurd that became an increasing part of American life at this time. *Catch-22* was followed swiftly by novels like Ken Kesey's *One Flew Over the Cuckoo's Nest* (1963), which also depicts a rebel hero at odds with the establishment, represented here by the insane asylum in which he finds himself; later novels like Thomas Pynchon's *The Crying of Lot 49* (1966), depict a comic version of America infected by dark conspiracies that generate paranoia at every turn. Towards the end of the decade books such as Kurt Vonnegut's *Slaughterhouse Five* (1969) also employ black humour and absurdity to relate their author's real life war experiences. So *Catch-22* appeared at the beginning of a period of change in American letters, as dark humour becomes a recurring, perhaps even dominant aesthetic, and the themes of social estrangement and paranoia are constantly revisited.

## 2.8 Heller after Catch-22

There was a sense in which, regardless of what Heller published in the future, nothing would ever equal the achievement of his first novel for many readers. Famously, when Heller was once asked why he hadn't published anything to equal *Catch-22*, he replied, 'Who has?'—which must rank as one of the great ripostes in literary history.[1] Yet Heller produced a significant body of work before his death in 1999, and at least two of his later novels, *Something Happened* (1974) and *Good as Gold* (1979), deserve to be considered alongside the best twentieth century American writing. The former is the story of Bob Slocum, a middle class working man preoccupied with the routines of work and the possibility of promotion; the latter's hero, Bruce Gold, is an academic and writer who strives to establish himself in politics. Despite obvious differences, numerous critics have seen parallels between these novels and the themes of *Catch-22*. For instance, Wayne C. Miller argues that:

> His heroes—Yossarian, Slocum, and Gold—all deal with the

---

[1] See Peter Kemp, ed., *The Oxford Dictionary of Literary Quotations* (Oxford: Oxford University Press,1997) 303

tangle of temptations that America, at the time of its ascendance, presents. All try to come to terms with themselves in a system wherein the power morality of the nation-state, that web of shifting alliances based on self-interest, has filtered down through the corporate order to family and individual relationships as well.[1]

The protagonists in his three great novels find themselves in environments where the systems that govern their lives—the world of the military, business, or politics—are seen as corrupt and self-serving. In each case the system sustains itself at the expense of the individual. While Yossarian is only able to free himself by opting out of the system, Bob Slocum doesn't have that privilege. As Miller suggest, *Something Happened*, 'permits no such illusion of escape. Slocum, defined primarily by his place in the economic order, is confined within the system that produced him.' And even though *Good as Gold* is a more upbeat novel than the latter, Heller 'is not able to offer his hero the hope in a political solution' here either, and the corruption is set to persist (Miller, 'Ethnic Identity as Moral Focus,' 4).

Some of the material that Heller produced later in life was less well received. *Picture This* (1988), for instance, was met with bafflement from most critics, and many thought his sequel to *Catch-22*, *Closing Time* (1994), to be a huge error on the author's part: for some the book is so weak that it could only harm Heller's standing as a writer. Despite the cool reviews, Heller continued to be a huge figure on the literary landscape right up to his death, and this has much to do with the enduring appeal of the novel which made him famous.

While *Catch-22* established his literary career, the effects on Heller's personal life were not all positive. There is evidence that he succumbed to the temptations that accompany celebrity—he had a number of affairs, for instance, something which resulted in the breakdown of his marriage to Shirley after 36 years. As one gossip columnist put it, '*Catch-22* may have been the beginning of the end of the marriage of Joseph and Shirley Heller' (Quoted in Daugherty, *Just One Catch*, 389). An extremely acrimonious divorce followed.

---

1 Wayne C. Miller, 'Ethnic Identity as Moral Focus: A Reading of Joseph Heller's *Good as Gold*,' *MELUS*, Vol. 6, No. 3, (Autumn, 1979), pp. 3–17 (3)

When Heller contracted Guillain-Barre syndrome in 1981, he developed a strong relationship with the nurse assigned to treat him, Valerie Humphries, and he eventually married her in 1987. He writes about this period of his life, specifically his illness and convalescence, in a book called *No Laughing Matter* (1986), co-authored with a close friend who also assisted Heller's recuperation, Speed Vogel.

Heller continued to write in the final years of his life, producing a memoir, *Now and Then*, in 1998, and a novel, *Portrait of an Artist as an Old Man*, another comparatively minor work, published posthumously in 2000. The memoir is interesting mainly because of the insights it offers into the apparent difficulty Heller had talking about his life outside of fiction. Peter Guttridge says of *Now and Then*, that Heller 'is more forthcoming about what he earned at different times in his life than about his own children.'[1] As with many writers it seems that, while inclined to be circumspect in his autobiography, he was much more candid about his life and relationships in his fiction. As suggested, he draws heavily on his own experiences for many episodes in *Catch-22*, and according to his daughter, *Something Happened* had 'years of verbatim conversations contained in it,' and revealed intimate aspects of her relationship with her father that she found deeply distressing (Erica Heller, *Yossarian Slept Here*, 131). It appears that Heller's own life and personality are at the heart of most of his fiction, not least *Catch-22*.

---

1 Peter Guttridge, 'Joseph Heller Obituary,' *The Independent*, Wednesday 15 December 1999. See bibliography for the web address.

# 3. Literary strategies

## 3.1. Humour in Catch-22

*Catch-22* is obviously a comic novel, and its humour is doubtless one of the factors contributing to its astounding commercial success: the comedy gives its 'high culture' themes more popular appeal than perhaps they might have had. As the English novelist Howard Jacobson says in his introduction to the 50th anniversary edition of the novel, *Catch-22* is

> Positioned teasingly [...] between literature and literature's opposites—between Rabelais and Dickens and Dostoevsky and Gogol and Celine and the Absurdists and of course Kafka on the one hand, and on the other, vaudeville and slapstick and Bilko and Abbott and Costello and Tom and Jerry and the Goons[1]

He correctly sees that the book occupies ground between high culture and popular culture, incorporating elements of both. Like the high culture authors Jacobson mentions, Heller strives to comment on the human condition, but he employs humour that has much in common with the comic entertainments more associated with mass culture, like cartoons, sitcoms, and stand-up comedy. A number of critics, particularly in the years immediately following its publication, felt that the overt comedy did not sit well with its serious objectives, and undermined the moral import of the book. For instance, the *New York Times Book Review* called it 'an emotional hodgepodge,' and *The New Yorker* referred to its 'debris of sour jokes,' suggesting that ultimately 'Heller wallows in his own laughter and finally drowns in it' (see Heller, *Now and Then*, 222).

Heller claims that he did not originally set out to make his book

---

[1] Howard Jacobson, 'Introduction,' Joseph Heller, *Catch-22 50th Anniversary Edition* (London: Vintage, 2011) 521–531.

explicitly comic, and it surprised him when people began laughing out loud at draft chapters of the work in progress, as he says in one interview:

> I thought I was being humorous, but I didn't know I would make people laugh. In my apartment one day I heard this friend of mine in another room laughing out loud, and that was when I realized I could be comic. I began using that ability consciously—not to turn *Catch-22* into a comic work, but for contrast, for ironic effect.[1]

In using the terms 'contrast' and 'ironic effect,' Heller is referring to his attempts to offset tragedy with comedy, which is arguably one of the most striking aspects of the book. In another interview he tells us that:

> I did consciously try to use a form of what might be called dramatic counterpoint, so that certain characters suffer tragedies, and they're dismissed almost flippantly—a line or two might describe something terrible happening to a character, whereas whole pages might be concentrated on something of *subordinate* dramatic value. And by doing that I tried to do two things. One was to emphasise the sense of loss, or sense of sorrow, connected with it; and also to capture this thing in experience which permits us to survive the loss of people who are dear to us. So that nobody's suffering lingers with us very long[2]

By refusing to elaborate on the demise of characters, by moving on swiftly after referencing a tragedy, he attempts to reflect the experience of loss: the sudden void that opens in our lives when someone we are close to dies. It is something he admired in the work of writers like Vladimir Nabokov and Evelyn Waugh, both of whom often move abruptly from a dark to a flippant tone. Heller seems to feel that his method of juxtaposing comedy and tragedy merely reflects the reality of life, which invariably combines the two; apparently he assumes that laughter functions as a coping mechanism that people fall back on when tragedy strikes.

---

1 George Plimpton, ed., 'Joseph Heller,' *Writers at Work: The Paris Review Interviews*. (London: Penguin, 1983) 231–248 (239).
2 Paul Krassner, 'Impolite Interview with Joseph Heller,' *The Realist*, #39, November 1962. For web address see bibliography.

## 3.2. The Structure and Realism in Catch-22

Anarchic humour is in keeping with Heller's desire to create a sense of instability and absurdity in his fictional universe. It complements our impression of Yossarian's world as topsy turvy: he exists in in an environment where innocent men are arrested, bombers bomb their own airbase, and the living are judged to be dead. This feeling of madness, chaos and confusion is complemented also by the structure of the book, which undermines linear narrative. As Heller says in interview with Paul Krassner:

> It's a novel that intentionally reverses the conventions of storytelling, which is to familiarise the reader with the essential facts of the narrative, the location, the character, what it's about; whereas I deliberately inverted, creating confusion, for about sixty, eighty pages.[1]

The book is disorientating at first partly because reference is made to characters and events that are not fully developed until later in the story. Jan Solomon writes that:

> Yossarian, like many other anti-heroes of modern fiction [...] lives in a world dominated not by chronological but by psychological time. Yossarian's time is punctuated, if not ordered, by the inexorable increases in the number of missions and by the repetitious returns to the relative safety and sanity of the hospital.[2]

Solomon means that the narrative is structured around issues and events that have significance for Yossarian, and these are not presented as they have unfolded in time, but more in terms of how they relate to Yossarian's state of mind. Snowden's death, for instance, precedes much of the action, but it is such a traumatic episode that it cannot be confronted fully at first: it is revealed gradually in the form of allusions and references that eventually become more detailed. In one sense, then, the narrative is deliberately confusing, and when we

---

[1] Charles Ruas, 'Joseph Heller Interview,' Adam J. Sorkin, ed., *Conversations with American Writers* (London: Quartet, 1986) 143–179 (152).

[2] Jan Solomon, 'The Structure of Joseph Heller's *Catch-22*.' In Harold Bloom ed., Bloom's *Modern Critical Interpretations: Joseph Heller's Catch-22* (New York: Bloom's Literary Criticism An imprint of Infobase Publishing, 2008) 56–65 (56)

begin the book we have to trust that the narrator will unpack and explain the details eventually; this is what happens, of course, and by the time we finish the novel it is possible to reassemble events in a chronological way, and see how everything fits together. The story takes place roughly over the course of a year, beginning late in 1943 with Yossarian being sent overseas, and ending in October 1944 with Yossarian's desertion. The hero's trajectory, when extracted from the convoluted structure, can be arranged as a linear and logical narrative, with a sequential beginning middle and end.

There is a parallel between the strange experience of reading the book, i.e. our initial sense of bewilderment as we proceed, and Yossarian's feeling of confusion and dislocation in the illogical environment of the airbase. According to Heller, one reason for creating this parallel was to reflect the nature of post-war America; he says that the structure of the novel 'derives from our present atmosphere, which is one of chaos, of disorganisation, of absurdity' (Paul Krassner, 'An Impolite Interview with Joseph Heller'). In another sense it could be seen as an appropriate representation of the experience of war, which is also often chaotic, disorganised and absurd; in other words, despite the novel's surrealism and comedy, there is an element of realism here; in fact, Robert Brustein argues that his method is *more* realistic than conventional realism, and that Heller 'manages to heighten the macabre obscenity of total war much more effectively through its gruesome comic aspects than if he had written realistic descriptions.'[1] Perhaps Heller captures the experience of war, then, despite the fact that the novel differs from what might be called documentary realism (in other words from novels such as *The Naked and the Dead,* mentioned above).

Heller is not really interested in the type of realism which purports to offer a window on reality, or which tries to convince the reader that they are reading anything other than fiction. Yet he still thinks of his work as expressing a kind of truth, as he makes clear in an interview with Creath Thorne:

---

1   Robert Brustein, 'The Logic of Survival in a Lunatic World.' In Harold Bloom, ed., *Bloom's Modern Critical Interpretations: Joseph Heller's Catch-22.* (New York: Bloom's Literary Criticism An imprint of Infobase Publishing, 2008) 3–8 (7)

> I like to regard a work of literature as a work of literature—as symbolic masquerade for reality. The reality and our writing about reality are two different things. There's something artificial in writing. Writing is different from life. A story about life is not the same as life itself […] In my books there is literal truth and there is imaginary truth, and hallucination is dealt with and fantasy is dealt with, interchangeably and simultaneously. It implies a recognition on my part, an admission on my part, that I'm telling you a story.[1]

He is not concerned with literal truth or fact, or in pretending that such a thing can even be conveyed in fiction, and as we read *Catch-22* it quickly becomes apparent that this world does not scrupulously correspond to our own. Things are taken to ridiculous extremes, characters behave in bizarre ways, and the world is sometimes cartoonlike. People do not actually behave this way. In the context of comedy, however, the demand for exact realism is relaxed, and the fact that the story is not lifelike in a conventional sense does not preclude the possibility of significance; in other words, the fact that the story does not attempt to accurately reproduce reality does not mean that it cannot have a bearing on reality. This is what Heller means by 'symbolic masquerade for reality;' he suggests that his fictions deal in 'imaginary' as opposed to 'literal' truths—things that cannot literally happen, but which nevertheless have relevance to our lives. In another interview Heller admits that his talent is not really suited to the kind of realism which relies on descriptive narrative:

> I can be humorous in several ways—with irony, with dialogue, with farcical situations, and occasionally with a lucky epigram or an aphorism […] But on the other hand, I cannot write an effective, straightforward, separate narrative. I can't write description. I've told my editor that I couldn't write a good descriptive metaphor if my life depended on it. In *Catch-22* there is really very little physical description.[2]

---

1  Creath Thorne, 'Joseph Heller: An Interview.' Adam J. Sorkin, ed., *Conversations with American Writers* (London: Quartet, 1986) 127–134 (132).
2  George Plimpton, 'Joseph Heller,' *Writers at Work: The Paris Review Interviews*, 237.

Though the novel is situated very specifically in terms of period and location, there is precious little descriptive detail to create a convincing sense place. He is not good at writing it, but he does not need it because, as suggested, it was not Heller's intention to write only about the War in this book: he was largely writing about modern America, and the lack of descriptive detail actually *helps* him do this because, in a manner of speaking, it works to free the events of the story from a specific location:

> When I was writing *Catch-22*, so much of it I saw as being related, not to World War II but to the domestic situation here, the political situation. It was the Korean War and the cold war. And I did not have a feeling that I was writing about World War II. Very little was said about World War II in *Catch-22*, other than that fascists are bad, and that's it. Most of the polemic that is there, and the topical humour, related to events occurring after World War II, during the McCarthy period [...] It's the absence of specific details which I think gives it that sense of application for today.[1]

So, according to Heller, the chaos and absurdity of Yossarian's war, reflected in the narrative's bizarre humour and 'inverted' structure, echoes events in modern America, specifically the period when Heller was writing the novel through the 1950s, and the lack of specific detail in *Catch-22* allows it to transcend its original context.

### 3.3. Influences

As suggested above, the writers who Heller feels influenced his writing in *Catch-22* are those associated less with traditional realism and more with surrealism, absurdity, satire and dark humour; principally: Louis-Ferdinand Céline, William Faulkner, Jaroslav Hašek, Franz Kafka, Vladimir Nabokov, Evelyn Waugh and Nathaniel West. These are very different writers, and Heller's fiction does not emulate any one of them in an obvious way. One specific novel that Heller cites as an influence is Hašek's *The Good Soldier Schweik* (1930); while,

---

1 Charles Ruas, 'Joseph Heller Interview,' *Conversations with American Writers*, 151–152.

again, this book is different in many ways, there are some similarities worth mentioning. For instance, one resemblance is that neither novel overtly politicises war—war is seen as meaningless in both, not linked, in other words, to a broader context that might make it morally explicable. *Schweik* is set in WWI, *Catch-22* in WWII, but as far as the respective conflicts are concerned, the novels posit no right and wrong as such. Also, the heroes of both novels are concerned principally with staying alive: in their view dying in war is not heroic, and rational people should avoid it. As war is meaningless, and death in war is irrational, it follows that institutions which facilitate war-making—the army for instance—are automatically seen as irrational too. This creates a situation in both novels where the dissenting heroes, though perfectly rational to resist the system, are deemed to be behaving irrationally in the worlds they inhabit. This conflict between the hero and the system, and the issue of rationality, is of central importance to both books, then, and in this respect alone Hašek's novel must be considered a significant precursor.

Of those writers to have influenced the spirit or atmosphere of *Catch-22*, it is arguably the work of Kafka that seems the most significant. This is particularly true of the comically frustrating nature of Yossarian's quandary. Gore Vidal once said that the word 'Helleresque' could even become a substitute for 'Kafkaesque as a description of a particular kind of nightmare situation' (quoted in Peter Guttridge, 'Joseph Heller, Obituary'). Kafka's stories often create worlds which don't make sense, and where authority is exercised over people in arbitrary ways. No one can fathom the ruling empire in Kafka's story, *The Great Wall of China* (1917), for instance, and the heroes of novels like *The Trial* (1925) and *The Castle* (1926) embark on maddeningly futile quests for meaning. We feel that it will remain elusive, even if it exists, and this is the impression we get of the ultimate meaning of the illogical rule of *Catch-22*. The world is like a prison in Kafka's works, and his protagonists are like Yossarian, trapped by incomprehensible bureaucracy and seemingly senseless decrees. Like Kafka's heroes, Yossarian is riddled with anxiety and caught in an inexorable nightmare—in his case this is created by Colonel Cathcart and the inevitability of him raising the number of missions he has to fly.

The influence of Kafka can also be seen in the idea of people being charged with crimes they didn't commit, and which they do not even understand: this situation is the basis of Kafka's *The Trial*, where the hero, Joseph K., is accused of a mysterious offence in the first chapter; thereafter he spends the entire novel trying to defend himself against a crime he cannot fathom. This scenario clearly inspired Heller when he came to write the scenes where the chaplain is accused of stealing near the close of the book.

Towards the end of Heller's life a minor scandal broke in America when a front page article in the *Washington Post* drew attention to the similarities between *Catch-22* and a novel that was published exactly ten years before it: Louis Falstein's *The Sky Is a Lonely Place* (1951). The question of plagiarism was raised, although Heller claimed never to have heard of the book, which appeared in the States under the title *Face of a Hero*. There is no reason to believe that Heller was lying, and Falstein himself never complained, even though he lived to witness the success of *Catch-22*. However, though this novel can't be said to have influenced Heller, the similarities are so striking that it is worth mentioning. Falstein's story focusses on an American bomber crew flying out of Italy in WWII, and is structured around their various bombing missions. Like Yossarian, the hero—a Jewish gunner named Ben—often has cause to question the competence of the powers-that-be. This is particularly so when the men are sent on missions during heavy cloud cover, regardless of the huge risk to their safety. They are ordered to go because their superiors—the Italy-based American Air Force—are suffering from an 'an inferiority complex,' in comparison to the British Royal Air Force, who are deemed more successful and daring. Ben sounds strikingly like Yossarian when he says, 'one of these cloudy days this inferiority complex would be the death of me.'[1] There are other similarities too: Falstein's Sergeant Arthur Sawyer, for instance, behaves rather like Milo Minderbinder in the way he is able to appropriate army property for his own needs, 'diverting food to the black market in Mandia.' As with Minderbinder, 'For Sawyer the Army was not only a career,

---

[1] Louis Falstein. *The Sky Is a Lonely Place*. (London: Rupert Hart-Davis, 1951) 227

it was a good business.' One character sums it up neatly when he says, 'That's the Army for you! That's war for you! The suckers get shot at, the smart guys get rich' (Louis Falstein, *The Sky Is a Lonely Place*. 58-9). Falstein seems to have had a similar war experience to Heller, flying at roughly the same time in roughly the same geographical region, so it is hardly surprising to find parallels between these books. Even if Heller *had* read Falstein, there is no sense in which he could be considered guilty of plagiarism. Heller's treatment is markedly different in tone and style; indeed, Falstein's book has much more in common with the kind of conventional realism that Heller was looking to distance himself from in *Catch-22*. Perhaps because of this, *The Sky Is a Lonely Place* offers an interesting alternative perspective on the kind of experiences that inform Heller's treatment, and the book is certainly of interest to those students of *Catch-22* who want to deepen their understanding of the air-war, and the predicament of those who fought it.

# 4. *Catch-22* - Sequential Development and Analysis

### 4.1. Chapters One to Six

Chapter 1 introduces Yossarian, the hero of the novel, and we quickly begin learn something of his predicament. He is in hospital on a military airbase in Pianosa, not because he is ill, but because there is a war on and the hospital is a place of comparative safety. He spends his days censoring letters and signing those he bothers to read, 'Washington Irving'; when that becomes boring he begins signing them, 'Irving Washington.' Washington Irving (1783-1859) is a well-known nineteenth century American writer, author of classic tales like 'Rip Van Winkle' and 'The Legend of Sleepy Hollow.' It is typical of Yossarian's irreverence that he should have fun with this name. The implication that a deceased fiction-maker is responsible for censoring the letters makes the point that censorship itself creates a fiction, and it provides an early example of how truth can be corrupted in the world of the novel. It also demonstrates Yossarian's status as a rebel, of course, and in this respect he is similar to his friend Dunbar, who is also residing in the hospital in order to avoid the war.

    The opening line of the novel also introduces Chaplain Tappman, a self-effacing Anabaptist who is visiting the patients on the ward. Yossarian claims to have fallen 'madly in love' with him because he is so 'sweet' and unassuming;[1] we later learn that he values him because he is caring, sensitive, and ethically driven, and these are rare traits in the world Yossarian inhabits. He and Dunbar are less charmed by the Texan who also joins them on the ward as a patient. Despite being 'good natured, generous, and likable' (*Catch-22*, 16), everyone hates him, partly because his patriotism is shot through

---

[1] Joseph Heller, *Catch-22*, (London: Corgi, 1981; first published by New York: Simon & Schuster, 1961) 13. All future references will be to the Corgi edition.

with a disagreeable élitism: he is someone who thinks that people with money should be given more votes than people without, and he is so annoying that he drives everyone out of the hospital, despite its status a safe haven. So there is an interesting distinction between two uses of the word 'good' here: while ostensibly it applies to both the chaplain *and* the Texan, as far as Yossarian is concerned it is only valid in relation to the former. The fact that the word 'good' is shown to be ambiguous suggests a potential distinction or slippage between language and reality—words in this novel are often contradictory and misleading, and in the very first pages of the book we learn that they should not be relied upon to communicate the truth.

Our impression of Yossarian as an alienated individual is developed in the second chapter as he recalls a dispute he once had with Officer Clevinger. Yossarian is scared because he feels everyone is trying to kill him, but Clevinger points out there is a war on and, as he puts it, 'They're trying to kill everyone' (*Catch-22*, 24). Yossarian cannot help but see the war in personal terms, even though Clevinger considers him crazy for doing so. Yossarian thinks everyone else is crazy, and that he is one of the few sane people he knows: 'Everywhere he looked was a nut, and it was all a sensible young gentleman like himself could do to maintain his perspective amid so much madness' (*Catch-22*, 28). The theme of sanity versus madness is clearly a feature here; each thinks the other is crazy, and this term is reiterated throughout the novel, forcing us, among other things, to ponder the notion of sanity and the relationship between reason and warfare. Yossarian finds it maddeningly difficult to convince people of the logic of his position and, as the novel develops, this contributes to his feelings of frustration and disaffection.

Chapters 3, 4 and 5 introduce further eccentrics like Orr, who teases Yossarian with seemingly pointless stories, and Chief White Halfoat who cannot settle in any one location because oil is always discovered wherever he resides. Then there is Hungry Joe who, after finishing his allotted number of bombing missions, lies 'screaming in his sleep every night' (*Catch-22*, 33). He does so because he knows the number of missions he must fly will be increased again by Colonel Cathcart, the imbecilic and dangerously ambitious leader of the squadron. Cathcart wants to become a general and he thinks he can impress his superiors by volunteering his men for extra duty. Yossarian is dismayed by this and longs for the camp doctor, Doc Daneeka, to ground him for being crazy, insanity being an apparent route out of combat duty. While there are many who will attest to Yossarian's craziness, he cannot be grounded because of Catch-22. The catch states that, while it is possible to ground crazy people, they have to formally declare themselves too crazy to fly, and in so doing they automatically reveal themselves as sane:

> 'You mean there's a catch?'
> 'Sure there's a catch,' Doc Daneeka replied, 'Catch-22. Anyone who wants to get out of combat isn't crazy.'
> There was only one catch and that was Catch-22, which specified that a concern for one's own safety in the face of dangers that were real and immediate was the process of a rational mind [...] Yossarian was moved very deeply by the absolute simplicity of this clause of Catch-22 and let out a respectful whistle (*Catch-22*, 54).

Catch-22, as it is expressed here, is essentially a verbal trick: it depends on a general definition of the word 'crazy' which fails to distinguish between medical and conversational uses; in other words, it fails to distinguish between applications that denote clinical insanity, and those that may not. In the real world this is a distinction that the military would be obliged to make, of course, and the Catch is not meant to be a realistic representation of a genuine regulation. It functions as a metaphor in the novel, creating a paradox or circular argument that reminds us how linguistic ambiguities can be exploited and abused. One of the implications, perhaps, is that power resides with those who have the capacity to manipulate language to their own ends.

In Chapter 6 we see that Catch-22 has other applications, and consequences. Despite the fact that Air Force Headquarters only expects men to fly forty missions, they are still not free to go home because the Catch states that the order of a commanding officer outweighs the regulation. As Daneeka explains,

> Even if the colonel were disobeying a Twenty-seventh Air Force order by making you fly more missions, you'd still have to fly them, or you'd be guilty of disobeying an order of his. And then Twenty-seventh Air Force Headquarters would really jump on you (*Catch-22*, 68).

We begin to get the impression that Catch-22 can mean what the people in authority want it to mean. Certainly numerous commentators have pondered the meaning of Heller's Catch over the years: Constance Denniston deems it 'a Fascistic rule [...] which forces [men] to do what they do not want to do;' Vance Ramsey calls it, 'that rider which seems to be attached to every code of the right of man and which gives those in authority the power to revoke those rights at will;' Jesse Ritter sees it as, 'the Absurd law of life [that] comes to designate all absurdity [...] from human to cosmic;' for John Hunt it is, 'the rule of discontinuity [...] the pandemic paradox of evil;' and for Jean Kennard it is an 'illustration of the irrational nature of the world.'[1] Catch-22 works in various ways in the book, but it is perhaps most simply expressed as the equivalent of a no-win situation, this is what it has come to denote for most people who use the phrase these days.

While Yossarian and Dunbar are traumatised by the prospect of flying missions, some of their fellow airmen seem to revel in it. Captain Havermeyer, for instance, is 'a lead bombardier who never missed,' and who approaches his targets fearlessly, refusing to take evasive action to avoid flak from German gunners, even though it puts him and his flight crew at risk. It's hardly surprising that the men prefer to fly behind Yossarian, who cares little for hitting the target, and whose primary purpose is 'to live forever or die in the attempt' (*Catch-22*, 37). Appleby is another pilot who thrives; he is good at everything and follows orders happily. Yossarian's own occasional pilot, McWatt, is another who remains cheerful in the face of imminent destruction; ostensibly he is perfectly sane, and hence as far as Yossarian is concerned he is 'the craziest combat man of them all' (*Catch-22*, 69). McWatt is more likeable than Havermeyer

---

1 All quoted in H.R. Swardson, 'Sentimentality and the Academic Tradition.' *College English*, 37, 8, 1976, 747–766, 749.

or Appleby, and Yossarian counts him among his friends, despite his recklessness; but the fact that an apparently sane man can act against his own self-interest with such enthusiasm is important in relation to the issue of sanity and madness: once more the distinction between them is problematized.

**4.2. Chapters Seven to Thirteen**

In Chapters 7, 8 and 9 we are introduced to other key characters such as Milo Minderbinder, Lieutenant Scheisskopf, and Major Major. Milo is a mess officer who is continually involved in profit making of various kinds; he is impressed with Yossarian when he first meets him, and is keen to go into partnership with him when he learns he can get as much free fruit as he wants thanks Doc Daneeka's decision to prescribe him an unlimited supply. Fanatically entrepreneurial, Milo is a ruthless genius whose commercial ambition is by turns hilarious and terrifying.

Lieutenant Scheisskopf is another obsessive: he is weirdly preoccupied with his cadets' marching prowess and their ability to win the red pennant award for the most adept marching performance at Sunday parades. He harbours a hatred for Clevinger and, while the latter was at cadet school, managed to get him tried. The incident makes Clevinger realise that it is possible for his own comrades to hate him even more than the Germans do, and the novel makes the point that hatred is not confined to ideological conflict: it is rife, irrational, and indiscriminate. Translated, Scheisskopf's name is 'shithead', and he is seen as feeble minded and fixated; his pathological obsession with parades is pointless and self-serving, and his loathing for Clevinger is pure malevolence. The fact that he is eventually promoted to the rank of general, despite being insane, offers its own comment on the military hierarchy.

Major Major, while not an overtly malicious character, is another inept leader. He is a hapless man, blighted by a resemblance to Henry Fonda, and by being promoted to squadron commander against his will whilst still in basic training. Looking like Henry Fonda leads to suspicion among some of the men that he really *is* Henry Fonda, and his premature promotion alienates him from those who resent his rank. Like Scheisskopf, and indeed like many other characters in the novel, the fact that he achieves elevated status despite his deficiencies is an indictment of a system that we're meant to see as run by incompetents: where some are promoted as a result of fierce ambition, however, Major Major is promoted thanks to an IBM computer 'with a sense of humour.' He compounds his isolation by agreeing to see people only when he is out if his office—in other words declining all appointments—and, inspired by Yossarian's joke in the hospital, spends his days signing documents with the name Washington Irving. The fact that he is occupied by such a pointless activity seems to have no discernible effect on the function of the base, suggesting that some administrative tasks are performed just for the sake of it.

Someone else who engages in a futile activity is Ex-P.F.C. Wintergreen, a character introduced in Chapter 10. He keeps going AWOL, and as punishment is stripped of his rank and 'sentenced to dig and fill up holes six feet deep.' He is happy enough in his role as it is safely away from the war in Colorado; more importantly, Wintergreen is an extremely influential individual despite his low rank: as the mail clerk at Headquarters he is able to forge documents, intercept mail and manipulate the system. The power he wields attests to the importance of controlling information in this organization, and suggests that those who think they're in charge, and who indeed *should* be in charge, are not.

Another character who, like Lieutenant Scheisskopf, hates people for no reason is Captain Black. He loathes the men generally, and is pleased that Cathcart keeps increasing the missions, particularly when he volunteers them for an extremely dangerous operation to Bologna. He is someone else obsessed with making himself look good in front of his superiors, and in Chapter 11 he instigates the Glorious Loyalty Oath Crusade in order to demonstrate the extent of his patriotism. This requires that the men pledge allegiance to their country by signing loyalty oaths whenever they pick up articles of kit; eventually this extends to the mess hall, and escalates to the point where they're forced to sing four choruses of *The Star Spangled Banner* before they are allowed to eat their food. He is frustrated in his ambition when

Major Major is promoted instead of him. Black is not on combat duty himself, so can luxuriate in his position of relative safety; his gloating and general misanthropy is another indication that the men face irrational hatred and hostility from the very forces that should be working to assist and protect them.

The bombing run to Bologna is a trip that most of the men are dreading. This is particularly true of Yossarian, who in Chapter 12 manages persuade Corporal Snark to put laundry soap in the men's food in order to give them diarrhea so they won't have to fly. He also moves the bomb line on the war map to suggest that the Allied forces have actually taken Bologna, rendering a mission unnecessary. As is often the case in *Catch-22*, when something appears on an official document it tends to be perceived as a literal fact—which is one of the reasons the mail clerk is so powerful, of course—and initially no one questions the change. While 'Moving the bomb line did not fool the Germans [...] it did fool Major ____ de Coverley,' the 'awe-inspiring, grave old man with a massive leonine head' who enters newly liberated cities in order to book recreational accommodation for officers and men (*Catch-22*, 144). Assuming it has been liberated, he embarks on such a mission to Bologna in Chapter 13, and disappears. He is a character of such forbidding aspect that everyone is frightened of him; indeed, no one is really sure what he does other than pitch horse shoes, and turn up in recently freed cities. Due to his high profile, the intelligence services of both the enemy and the allies are interested in establishing who he actually is, but cannot. The fact that he remains an enigma suggests a massive problem with the military as an institution: it is unfathomable even to its own intelligence service, who cannot explain the function of its own staff, let alone the enemy.

### 4.3. Chapters Fourteen to Twenty

Eventually the mission to Bologna has to be flown, and Chapters 14 and 15 relate this terrifying ordeal. Yossarian—who in his early career had been given a medal for flying over a target twice in order to be sure of destroying it—instructs his pilot, Kid Sampson, to return to base on the flimsy excuse of a broken intercom. When the rest of the planes return at the end of the mission, it appears that Bologna has been a 'milk run'—that is there was no enemy flak or resistance—and there have been no casualties. The following day the squadron embarks on another mission to Bologna with Yossarian as the lead bombardier. This time he 'came in on the target like a Havermeyer, confidently taking no evasive action at all;' however, it turns out they have been duped and 'suddenly they were shooting the living shit out of him.' Yossarian's reaction to this incident is interesting as it deepens our insight into his personality. While concerned with saving his own skin, he is also seen to be anxious about the wellbeing of his colleagues; he is anxious about the safety of Orr, for instance, the character whose infuriating personality drives him to distraction. Yossarian's compassion and capacity for empathy is an important facet of his personality, suggesting that he has a moral dimension. He is not motivated purely by self-interest, or by cowardice, a fact that makes it easier to identify and sympathize with him, and which distinguishes him from many others in the book.

The next chapter also extends our understanding of Yossarian. Following the Bologna ordeal he takes rest leave in Rome and meets Luciana, 'a buxom, delightful, flirtatious girl' (*Catch-22,* 166) whom he takes to dinner, but who refuses to sleep with him until the following morning, and only then when she has tidied his room up first. Their lovemaking is interrupted by Hungry Joe who bursts in on the couple in the hope of photographing them. This shows how Yossarian's life is subject to disruption and chaos even at moments when pleasure and happiness seem attainable. Despite the interruption, Yossarian and Luciana establish a significant bond, but the latter is cynical: she doesn't think Yossarian will bother to pursue the relationship once they part, and she tells him that he'll tear up her name and address the second he leaves: 'You'll tear it up into little pieces the minute I'm gone and go walking away like a big shot because a tall, young, beautiful girl like me, Luciana, let you sleep with her and did not ask you for money.' As soon as he is alone that is exactly what he does, 'feeling very much like a big shot because a beautiful young girl like Luciana had slept with him and did not ask for any money' (*Catch-22*, 176). He immediately regrets it, but again this tells us something significant about Yossarian, and perhaps about human nature in general. The act is patently against his self-interest, and the reader cannot help but feel that it constitutes exactly the kind of illogical behavior that the novel constantly satirizes and which blights Yossarian's existence. The book is forever making the point that Catch-22 is irrational, and that the military machine defies logic, but the same seems to be true of the hero's actions: it implies that a capacity for absurdity is pervasive, perhaps even inherent in the human condition.

Chapter 17 sees Yossarian back in the hospital, and effectively returns us to the beginning of the story and his encounter with the chaplain and the Texan. Here resides the mysterious soldier-in-white who spends his days immobile on his back with his limbs in casts, hoisted by wire cables; to his fellow patients he seems to be 'constructed entirely of gauze, plaster and a thermometer' (*Catch-22*, 181). This character is completely anonymous—there is even a suspicion that the cast may be empty, or that the soldier inside, if there is one, may have perished. In this sense he can be seen to represent the dehumanizing nature of war, and the extent to which it deprives men of their identity. The nurses toil over him, changing his drip and polishing the pipe that is fixed to his groin, until one day they discover that he actually *is* dead. Death becomes a central theme of this chapter, with Yossarian making reference to the death of Snowden, the young man who died in his plane over Avignon. While there are a number of allusions to this incident at various points in the story, the full details are withheld until later in the book. In keeping with the death theme, this chapter also catalogues the various fatal diseases that worry Yossarian and Doc Daneeka; the latter even keeps lists of them 'in alphabetical order so that he could put his finger without delay on any one he wanted to worry about' (*Catch-22*, 186). Daneeka is as paranoid about dying as Yossarian, and he is so scared of flying that Yossarian arranges for his name to be forged in the flight log so that he can collect his flight pay without having to spend time in the air.

The theme of death continues in Chapters 18 and 19, where it is addressed alongside the issue of religion. Yossarian is asked to pose as the dying son of a family who has flown all the way from New York to be at his deathbed. This is a funny, oddly touching scene in which the family is certain their son will soon be going to heaven. His father instructs him to tell 'the man upstairs' that 'it ain't right for people to die when they're young,' and his brother advises him not to let anyone push him around in heaven just because he is Italian (*Catch-22*, 201). Theirs is a comically unsophisticated conception of heaven that reflects their earthly fears and preoccupations. The scene follows a section in which Yossarian recollects a conversation he once had about religion with Lieutenant Scheisskopf's wife. They both agree that they are atheists, but when Yossarian begins attacking the concept of God, suggesting that such an omnipotent creator must be cruel, vengeful and abhorrent, she becomes furious on the grounds that 'the God I don't believe in is a good God, a just God, a merciful God. He's not the mean and stupid God you make him out to be' (*Catch-22*, 195). Just as the concept of God provides comfort for the bereaved family whose son Yossarian impersonates, so it does for Scheisskopf's allegedly atheistic wife. It is important to note that the terms in which she expresses this are clichés, of course, suggesting a superficial, unthinking acceptance of a benign deity.

Chapter 19 presents a slightly different take on the same issue. Here we are offered a more detailed insight into Colonel Cathcart's personality, and we learn that he is 'an industrious, intense, dedicated military tactician who calculated day and night in the service of himself' (*Catch-22*, 203); he is also a status obsessed, paranoid bully who browbeats those of inferior rank. In this chapter Cathcart discusses with the chaplain the possibility of beginning each mission with a prayer. This isn't because he thinks it will benefit the men, but because he believes it may qualify him for a feature in *The Saturday Evening Post*, and as a consequence boost his profile and career. He begins to question the wisdom of his idea when he learns what tone the prayers might take:

> 'Haven't you got anything humorous that stays away from waters and valleys and God? I'd like to keep away from the subject of religion altogether if we can.'

> The chaplain was apologetic. 'I'm sorry, sir, but I'm afraid all the prayers I know are rather somber in tone and make at least some passing reference to God' (*Catch-22,* 207).

Cathcart is interested in religion only insofar as it can serve his interests, and he has no depth of understanding of its values or its implications; the only thing he seems certain of is that everyone should believe in it. When the chaplain tells him that they may be obliged to excuse atheists from any prayer meetings he refuses to believe that such views exist in his outfit: 'Atheism is against the law isn't it?' he asks.

While there is no questioning the chaplain's sincerity, he is presented as a rather weak man who is having something of a crisis of faith himself. In Chapter 20 we see how he lets himself be bullied by his assistant, Corporal Whitcomb, with whom he shares a tent. Despite being inferior in rank, Whitcomb is insubordinate and openly hostile to the chaplain. He plots against him, telling a C.I.D. man that the chaplain is the one responsible for signing 'Washington Irving' on official documents. Later in the novel he goes behind his back to Colonel Cathcart with the idea of sending comforting letters to the families of deceased servicemen. Cathcart is happy to embrace this because—after the failure of the prayers-before-missions idea—he thinks *this* might be the story to get his name in *The Saturday Evening Post*. So while the chaplain is a decent and likeable man, he is also rather pathetic and spineless: he is unwilling to stand up for himself, and few people take him seriously as a result. So in some ways the novel is quite dismissive of religion—men like Cathcart are only interested in how it can be used to promote their own interests, while people like Mrs Scheisskopf and the Italian family have a naïve and childish understanding of God. In this respect it is important that Yossarian—who is overtly hostile to religion—has that ethical dimension mentioned earlier, because it suggests that people don't need religion in order to think and behave morally; Yossarian might be an atheist but his sense of right and wrong is as well-defined as anyone's.

## 4.4. Chapters Twenty One to Twenty Seven

By Chapter 21 Colonel Cathcart is becoming increasingly conscious of Yossarian as a problem in his life. His name keeps cropping up as someone intent on making trouble for him. Yossarian has been complaining about the missions the men are expected the fly, for instance, and he also appeared naked to receive his medal after the mission to Avignon. It was on this mission that Snowden was killed: he bled all over Yossarian's uniform and now he has vowed never to wear one again. Cathcart suspects that it was also Yossarian who moved the bomb line on the map, and who started an episode of moaning during the briefing before the Avignon mission. Yossarian was overcome with desire for General Dreedle's nurse and, as his lustful groan became infectious, some of the other men joined in. This infuriated General Dreedle who insisted the men desist, and even threatened to shoot Major Danby when he let out an unintentional moan. This comical scene underscores our sense of Yossarian's frustration: in the presence of a beautiful woman a healthy young man like him should be following his instincts and his libido, rather than setting out to face death. We also begin to see that Yossarian is becoming difficult to control; his dissent is beginning to register with the powers-that-be and it is clear that he is heading for a conflict with them; we get the impression that he finds it hard to govern himself, and our anticipation of the inevitable forthcoming conflict creates narrative tension.

Yossarian's dread of the Avignon assignment is well founded because, as suggested, it is on this mission that his plane is hit by flak and Snowden loses his life. The episode has been foreshowed in earlier chapters, but is narrated in greater detail in Chapter 20 two where it is described as 'the mission on which Yossarian lost his nerve [...] because Snowden lost his guts' (*Catch-22*, 241). Interestingly, when Yossarian's plane goes into a dive, the avowed atheist responds by screaming, '*Oh God! Oh God! Oh God! Oh God!*' —yet another contradiction in a book full of logic-defying contradictions! The various references to Snowden's death that precede this chapter have served to create a degree of intrigue around it, and here the mystery is partly resolved: we see how Snowden died, and hence why Yossarian appears naked to receive his medal. As suggested, Yossarian clearly has the ability to be affected by human suffering, but his response to Snowden's death isn't solely due to compassion: the incident has also increased Yossarian's sense of his own mortality. As the novel develops we see that while Yossarian possesses many laudable and noble characteristics, he is a morally complex person. This is seen in his attitude to a potential plan to kill Colonel Cathcart hatched by his co-pilot on the Avignon mission, Dobbs. All Dobbs requires in order to go ahead and kill Cathcart is Yossarian's endorsement, but at the outset Yossarian refuses to give it. At this stage at least, he can't bring himself to sanction murder, even if it is Cathcart, an individual who threatens the life of himself, and every other airman on the base. Later in the novel, however, when Cathcart continues to increase the missions, Yossarian changes his mind. In other words, Yossarian is not a saint, and when Cathcart comes to seem a bigger threat to Yossarian than the Nazis, he is willing to sanction murder. Perhaps the fact that self-preservation ultimately takes precedence over morality for Yossarian makes him a more realistic, variegated character.

Chapter 22 also develops the character of Milo Minderbinder. Yossarian and Orr accompany him on a rest leave trip to Cairo to purchase eggs, and they end up doing a tour of Southern Europe, North Africa and the Middle East as Milo tirelessly moves from one place to another, buying and selling goods. They find that he is revered wherever he goes. He has been elected Mayor of Palermo, and Assistant Governor General of Malta; he is also Vice-Shah of Oran, 'Caliph of Bagdad, the Imam of Damascus, and the Sheik of Araby' (*Catch-22*, 254). He is lauded in such places because he is perceived to have boosted their economies; and the bewildering deals he manages to pull-off are astonishingly successful, even as they seem to defy logic. Milo is worshipped the way money is worshipped; indeed, the fact that he is an Iman, and is revered as a god in parts of Africa, suggests how money can even take the place of religion in the world. The fickle nature of free enterprise is also indicated in this chapter as Milo is brought to the brink of ruin after he 'cornered the market on cotton that no one else in the world wanted' (*Catch-22*, 254). Milo is a despicable character in many ways, but the fact that Yossarian seems to like him complicates things for the reader; again, as with Dobb's plan to murder Cathcart, it might make us want to qualify our assessment of Yossarian and his judgement; once more it could be seen to amplify the moral complexity of the book, making the point that there are no simple answers to such questions.

Chapter 23 develops the character of Nately, a good-natured nineteen year old from a wealthy family. This friend of Yossarian is in love with a prostitute who doesn't return his affections, and he is rather naïve, particularly in regard to his unquestioning patriotism. At one point he has an argument with a cynical old man who openly admits to switching allegiances during the war for the sake of expediency. When Nately claims to be happy to risk his life for his country, the old man mocks him:

> 'What is a country? A country is a piece of land surrounded on all sides by boundaries, usually unnatural ... There are now fifty or sixty countries fighting this war. Surely so many countries can't all be worth dying for.'
> 'Anything worth living for,' said Nately, 'is worth dying for.'
> 'And anything worth dying for,' said the sacrilegious old man, 'is worth living for' (*Catch-22*, 261).

The old man expresses a philosophy not unlike Yossarian's here, and Nately's idealism seems rather empty in comparison. While the old man is ugly, lecherous, and amoral, Nately is handsome, well-mannered and principled, but it is difficult not to conclude that the former has the stronger argument.

Amorality becomes an issue in Chapter 24, where the focus returns to Milo. Despite the Egyptian cotton setback his business empire his now huge, and even the warplanes bear the logo: M&M Enterprises. Ostensibly he seems to be working for everyone's benefit, and he always insists that each person owns a share of the business. In this sense it can be seen as a parody of socialism as well as capitalism. Milo feels the fact the everyone has a share gives him licence to do anything to further his business interests, including making a deal with the Germans that involves him bombing his own camp. Milo is more like a capitalist in his view that money takes precedence over morality, as he tells Yossarian when justifying his deals with the enemy: 'Maybe they did start the war, and maybe they are killing millions of people, but they pay their bills more promptly than some allies of ours I could name' (*Catch-22*, 273). Initially people are outraged that Milo organised the bombing of his own men: 'Not one voice was raised in his defence.' But this changes when 'he opened his books to the public and disclosed the tremendous profit he made' (*Catch-22*, 276). The public's greed, and their gullibility, is being satirized here, of course, as well as Milo's voracious ambition.

Later in Chapter 24 Milo joins Yossarian at Snowden's funeral. Yossarian is still refusing to wear clothes and he observes the proceedings perched on the branch of a nearby tree. Milo has an idea for disposing of his useless Egyptian cotton by covering it in chocolate and serving it to the men in the mess halls—the fact that cotton is inedible seems unimportant to him. Again we see a character with uncritical faith in appearances: because chocolate covered candy sounds edible, he feels chocolate covered cotton must be. It is worth noting that Yossarian refers to the tree in which they sit both as 'the tree of life' and 'of knowledge of good and evil.' Despite Yossarian's atheism, these references have biblical connotations. Presumably they serve as a figurative vehicle for his reflections on life, death, and morality at this time of sadness. Milo's more literal reading of the tree, as 'a chestnut tree' (*Catch-22*, 279), is consistent with their differing personalities. Milo is a genius, in one sense, but his insistence on mundane fact here is indicative of the limited nature of his personality. Yossarian's perspective on the world is more capable of embracing metaphor: it is richer, subtler, more playful, and, as a consequence, more human.

The biblical references in this episode take on a deeper significance in Chapter 25. By this time the chaplain's crisis of faith is beginning to climax. He is upset when learns of his assistant, Whitcomb's, decision to go over his head to Colonel Cathcart about the letters of condolence, and he is distressed when Cathcart volunteers the men for the dangerous Avignon mission. The colonel wants as many casualties as he can get as soon as possible so that the letter-of-condolence scheme might get him into the Christmas edition of *The Saturday Evening Post*. The chaplain is angry and traumatised, then, and we are told that 'so many things were testing his faith;' indeed the chaplain would have forsaken his calling altogether had it not been for the seemingly miraculous visions he'd recently experienced. These faith-affirming 'mystical phenomena,' include 'the naked man in the tree at the poor sergeant's funeral' (*Catch-22*, 304). In other words, when the chaplain saw Yossarian naked in the tree, he thought he'd witnessed a divine vision. At this stage, all that sustains the chaplain's faith is not a mystical phenomenon (or miracle) at all, but the very mundane figure of his naked friend—whom he fails to recognise—at the end of *his* emotional tether. This can be seen as a comment people's ability to misread the facts in ways that suit their own beliefs and emotional needs. The chaplain is no different from the Italian family, who are willing to believe that Yossarian is their son and that he will soon be going to heaven; in short it suggests that people are all too willing to delude themselves.

Chapters 26 and 27 see Yossarian back in hospital yet again after being wounded in the leg on a mission. He and Dunbar change identities with some enlisted men after pulling rank on them and ordering them out of their beds: Dunbar becomes A. Fortiori, and Yossarian becomes Warrant Officer Homer Lumley; they enjoy switching about and the ability to exercise a degree of power. During his stay Yossarian is interviewed by a psychiatrist, Major Sanderson, and their exchange creates an excellent satire of psychiatry and those who practise it. Sanderson is obsessed with finding 'the true reason' behind Yossarian's unambiguous actions and straightforward answers to his questions; he reveals himself as neurotic, self-obsessed and, more importantly, in no position to judge his patients' sanity. Sanderson arbitrarily determines that Yossarian is psychologically unfit for duty, and signs the papers necessary to send him home. Unfortunately, because of the confusion created by the various identity switches, the psychiatrist believes that Yossarian is A. Fortiori, and Yossarian is foiled again by the system. Once more documentation carries more weight than reality; despite his protestations, A. Fortiori is sent home instead of Yossarian who, along with Dunbar, is promptly sent back into combat. This funny episode not only offers another indictment of blind bureaucracy, but proffers a fitting punishment on Yossarian for his decision to abuse his power by pulling rank. After all, the fact that he himself suffers as a consequence of such abuse suggests that he should know better.

**4.5. Chapters Twenty Eight to Thirty Five**

In Chapter 28 we learn more about Orr, an eccentric little man with peculiar features and impressive practical skills. Yossarian finds him by turns infuriating and endearing: Orr annoys Yossarian with his constant tinkering with mechanical devices such as the stove he is fixing in order to keep the tent warm, but he also feels protective towards him. Yossarian realizes that he is the type likely to be victimized by more athletic, good looking, and confident people like Appleby, and he feels 'a flood of compassion sweep over him' when he thinks of this (*Catch-22*, 332). Yossarian's need to protect Orr is a response to the degree of injustice and inequity he sees around him. Orr seems like the kind of person who is easily exploited and victimized. At the end of the novel, however, we learn that this is likely to have been a misreading of Orr, who seems to have been planning an ingenious escape all along. Still, as suggested, Yossarian's capacity to care about others clearly distinguishes him from characters like Cathcart and Milo. In this chapter we are told that Yossarian feels ashamed because he once asked never to be assigned to fly with Orr because Orr was always having accidents, ditching his planes in the sea and having to be rescued. Orr questions him about it and tries persuading Yossarian to change his mind. Unsurprisingly he will not, and when Orr once more ditches his plane and is lost at sea it appears as if he has made the right decision.

Lieutenant Scheisskopf re-enters the story in Chapter 29 when General Peckham transfers him from the American base to work on his staff. Scheisskopf is dismayed when he finds that he will not have the opportunity to organise parades, but Peckham is able to placate him by mentioning the military's new obsession with bomb patterns. These have no military significance, but 'have caught on,' particularly with Colonel Cathcart who embraces them because he thinks they please the General (*Catch-22,* 345). They attend a briefing for a mission to bomb an insignificant Italian village, and the men are uneasy as it will mean civilian losses even though the mission has no purpose other than to create a pointless roadblock. Colonel Korn offers them a choice between bombing this safe target or being sent once more on a flak-heavy mission to somewhere like Bologna. The men opt for the safe target, even after Korn admits that it's a completely meaningless mission:

> We don't care about the roadblock [...] Colonel Cathcart wants to come out of this mission with a good aerial photograph he won't be ashamed to send through channels (*Catch-22,* 348).

The mission's purpose, in other words, is to serve Cathcart's ego and ambition. As with Scheisskopf's marches, we observe a privileging of appearance over reality here. We have already seen how important appearances are in this world—people are all too willing to accept them uncritically, whether it is Yossarian's altered bomb-line or Milo's chocolate-covered candy.

This concept is developed in an even more dramatic way in Chapters 30 and 31. Yossarian's friend, McWatt, has a habit of flying his plane low over the beach of Pianosa in order to buzz the bathers; on one occasion Kid Sampson jumps up and tries to touch the plane and is cut in half by the propeller. McWatt, unable to face the consequences of his actions, flies the plane into a mountain and kills himself. It is mistakenly assumed the Doc Daneeka is on board because his name appears in the flight log, and he becomes officially listed as deceased. Official notification is sent to his wife, and Daneeka's pay is discontinued. Despite the fact that Daneeka is quite clearly alive, his colleagues on the base refuse to acknowledge it:

> Not even the chaplain could bring Doc Daneeka back to life under the circumstances. Alarm changed to resignation, and more and more Doc Daneeka acquired the look of an ailing rodent. The sacks under his eyes turned hollow and black, and he padded through the shadows fruitlessly like a ubiquitous spook (*Catch-22,* 366).

Just as image takes precedence over reality in Scheisskopf's parades and Cathcart's bomb patterns, so Doc Daneeka's official status has more weight than his literal status. Doc Daneeka's wife receives an insurance pay-out for her husband's death, and she and their children move out of their home without leaving a forwarding address. Though he may not be factually dead, Daneeka's life is effectively ruined: the culprit, of course, is bureaucracy, and people's willingness blindly to adhere to it.

Alongside all the references to death, we are never allowed to forget that Yossarian is a virile young man who is full of life. He begins a relationship with Nurse Duckett, and his desire for her, and his appreciation of her physicality and sensuality reminds us of his love and appreciation of life: this augments our sense of how precious it is, and how he is right to protect it. However, we do begin to see some ways in which the war is aging and diminishing Yossarian, particularly in Chapter 32 when a group of young soldiers are moved into his tent: their rambunctiousness and gullible enthusiasm for combat annoy him, making him feel like 'a crotchety old fogey of twenty eight' (*Catch-22*, 369). By this stage, of course, Yossarian is a seasoned airman who has witnessed the full horror of combat. He is offered the chance to move out of the tent but refuses, feeling that it would be a betrayal of his lost tent-mate, Orr. While Yossarian may have legitimate reasons for his inability to tolerate the young men, this episode is also an indication that all may not be well with his state of mind.

Chapter 33 sees Yossarian on leave in Rome. He misses Nurse Duckett intensely and searches in vain for satisfying female company. It is in this chapter that Nately's whore—who has previously treated Nately with contempt—finally falls in love with him: all she required for this change of heart was a good night's sleep. The fact that Yossarian's state of mind is deteriorating seems to be confirmed at the end of this chapter when we learn that he has broken Nately's nose and forced him into hospital. In the next chapter we find that this happened following a Thanksgiving Day party at the base when everyone was drunk on cheap whisky supplied by Milo. Some soldiers began shooting tracer fire over the camp as a joke, terrifying and enraging Yossarian who took his pistol and sought them out. When Nately tried to subdue his friend, Yossarian broke his nose. Of course Yossarian instantly regrets it, and he checks into the hospital alongside Nately to apologise. The chaos continues here, however, when Dunbar goes wild following the apparent return of the soldier-in-white—the anonymous patient who apparently died earlier in the book. Though it is accepted that this is a different soldier, Dunbar won't be pacified, and bedlam breaks loose on the ward. It takes several M.P.s to restrain Dunbar, and later Nurse Duckett warns Yossarian that they are going to 'disappear' his friend:

> 'What does that mean?'
> 'I don't know. I heard them talking behind a door.'
> 'Who?'
> 'I don't know. I couldn't see them. I just heard they were going to disappear Dunbar' (*Catch-22,* 389)

It is never clear what this means, but sure enough at the end of the chapter Dunbar is missing. So the notion that Yossarian is living in a world that is beyond his control, and which is indeed out of control, continues. Now not even the hospital can be seen as a safe haven. Everywhere he turns Yossarian's world is chaotic, and this chaos is fuelled by characters that are often on the verge of metal collapse; at the same time there is an increasing sense that malign forces are operating in the background. By Chapter 35 it is clear that Milo is one such force. In conversation with Colonel Cathcart, Milo manages to justify having the other men fly his missions for him in return for his enterprise (after all, they all have a share). Initially he appears to balk at lumbering his friend Yossarian in this way, but manages to use spurious verbal logic to absolve himself of responsibility:

> 'I'd give everything I owned to Yossarian,' Milo persevered gamely in Yossarian's behalf. 'But since I don't own anything, I can't give everything to him, can I? So he'll just have to take his chances with the rest of the men, won't he?' (*Catch-22,* 397).

Once more the people who thrive are those who can make language work for them. Just as Catch-22 can be used to ensnare the men with a verbal sleight-of-hand, so Milo can negate any obligation to

Yossarian, and exonerate himself morally in the course of a single sentence. While Milo might not technically own anything, he hardly seems to be working in the men's interest—he raises the price of food in his mess hall so high that all the officers and men have to turn their pay over to him in order to eat; but of course he can rationalize that too:

> Their alternative—there was an alternative, of course, since Milo detested coercion and was a vocal champion of freedom of choice—was to starve (*Catch-22*, 391).

The novel uses Milo to satirize the kind of logic occasionally used to justify political and economic systems that purport to offer choice, but in reality do not. Despite his rationalisations, and his appeals to equality and fairness, Milo thrives while others suffer, often as a direct consequence of his enterprise. Indeed, at the end of the chapter in which Milo frees himself from the responsibility of flying combat missions, more of Yossarian's friends are killed in action, including Dobbs, and Nately.

### 4.6. Chapters Thirty Six to Forty Two

Yossarian's world is beginning to unravel as Chapter 36 begins, and so is the chaplain's, who is also hit hard by Nately's death. This chapter sees him taken to a cellar and interrogated about signing official documents with the name Washington Irving, and of stealing a plum tomato from Colonel Cathcart's office. At first his accusers refuse to identify a charge, and they make it clear that the truth is irrelevant:

> 'That's a very serious crime you've committed, Father,' said the major.
> 'What crime?'
> 'We don't know yet,' said the colonel. 'But we're going to find out. And we sure know it's very serious' (*Catch-22*, 402).

This chapter is reminiscent of Kafka's *The Trial*, in which the hero, Josef K., is accused of an unspecified crime. As with Josef K., the chaplain's predicament is both comically absurd and horrifying, and it reflects the helplessness of those who find themselves at the mercy of an apparently irrational system. From what we have seen of the system by this stage, we are left in little doubt that it could easily define the innocent chaplain as a criminal, and justify just about any punishment. The chaplain is released, but with the threat of punishment for an unspecified crime hanging over him, and the warning that he is 'under surveillance twenty-four hours a day' (*Catch-22*, 409). Just to compound the sense of absurdity and injustice, in the following chapter we learn that the grossly incompetent Lieutenant Scheisskopf has been promoted to general. His first directive is for everyone to march, even though the inappropriateness and futility of this activity has already been established.

As if Yossarian wasn't in enough danger, another threat to his life emerges in Chapter 38 when Nately's whore decides to blame him for Nately's death. She attacks him viciously with a potato peeler, and he barely manages to escape with his life. By this stage Yossarian has reached his emotional nadir: his friends are dead, and everywhere he looks he can only see irrationality, injustice and gratuitous misanthropy. He refuses to fly any more combat missions and begins walking backwards with his gun on his hip in protest.

Chapter 39, entitled 'The Eternal City,' sees Yossarian absent without leave in Rome, and constitutes the culmination of his estrangement. All he encounters on the streets of the city are people being exploited and abused: he sees a dog mistreated, a woman raped, a small boy beaten by a man while a crowd fails to intervene. The chapter is influenced heavily by Dostoevsky's novel, *Crime and Punishment* (1866), and it also owes something to the Italian poet Dante. As Heller says in interview,

> It was a trip to the underworld, a purgation from which Yossarian emerges. Remember the last episode there. It has to do with a woman who Yossarian doesn't help. He is guilty and that is the beginning of his moral consciousness.[1]

So we are meant to see this as a moral turning point for Yossarian.

---

1  Richard B. Sale, 'An Interview in New York with Joseph Heller' in Adam J. Sorki, ed., *Conversations with Joseph Heller* (Mississippi: University Press of Mississippi, 1993) 78–90 (90).

Like Dante he has seen the 'underworld,' and the depths to which human beings can fall, and he has become conscious of his own moral shortcomings: now, like Dostoevsky's hero Raskolnikov, he must face up to this. His conscience has been pricked, and when Yossarian faces his next moral decision, he is in a position to make a more worthy choice.

Yossarian finds that the women of the brothel he used to frequent have been driven out and are now homeless. There doesn't seem to be any justification for this, and when Yossarian enquires he is told by the one old lady still in residence that, 'Catch-22 says they have a right to do anything and we can't stop them' (*Catch-22*, 430). He is incensed to hear yet another mention of this illogical decree, and though he questions the reality of its existence, he is forced to acknowledge its power:

> Catch-22 did not exist, he was positive of that, but it made no difference. What did matter was that everyone thought it existed, and that was much worse, for there was no object or text to ridicule or refute, to accuse, criticize, attack, amend, hate, revile, spit at, rip to shreds, trample upon or burn up. (*Catch-22*, 432).

This might suggest the extent to which people are complicit in their own oppression; rather than questioning the system, people too readily tolerate it, together with their role as victims. So this may be a criticism of people's passive willingness to accept the dictates of the powers-that-be; certainly there seems to be a readiness to assume that the law will always work in favour of authority rather than justice in the novel. Indeed, when Yossarian later returns to the Rome apartment he finds confirmation of this. Aarfy has raped and murdered a maid, an act he tries to justify by referring to her as a mere 'servant girl.' Outraged, Yossarian lectures him on morality, and when the M.P.s arrive he assumes they are there to arrest Aarfy; instead 'they arrested Yossarian for being in Rome without a pass,' and 'apologized to Aarfy for intruding' (*Catch-22*, 443). Yossarian is arrested for a petty crime whilst a murderer and rapist goes free—just one more injustice to compound Yossarian's impression that justice doesn't exist.

Despite his arrest, Chapter 39 ostensibly ends on a positive note for

Yossarian when Colonels Cathcart and Korn inform him that that he is about to be sent home. 'There was, of course, a catch,' and the following chapter makes clear exactly what this involves. The chapter is titled 'Catch-22', and here the catch becomes an 'odious' moral compromise for Yossarian. Cathcart and Korn will send him home only if he is prepared to pretend to like them, to be their pal. If he agrees they will send him home as a hero; if he refuses he will be court-martialled. Initially he agrees, but when he leaves their office he is attacked again by Nately's whore who stabs him and flees, and Chapter 41 sees Yossarian back in the hospital again. Here he relives Snowden's death once more, and at last—after so many previous references to the event—the final moments of his friend's life are described in protracted and graphic detail. The fact that this episode keeps resurfacing in Yossarian's mind underlines the point that he can't forget it. At the same time, the fragmented way that it has been presented up till now also suggests that he finds it painful to remember it. He has been unable to fully confront it, which is implied by the fact that previous references to the incident have been superficial compared to this one. The effect of this scene is to help make us aware of the consequences of war, and of the decisions made by the madmen who preside over men's lives. The novel takes a very dark turn in this chapter, then; but of course, given that this is a comic novel, former references to Snowden's death have occasionally been framed in a humorous context, and it is hard not to feel that this affects how we relate to it. For instance, the comedy that has accompanied references to Snowden's death up to this point might make the reader inclined to take it rather lightly, and hence not be as critical as they should be of those whose carelessness have contributed to the tragedy (namely people like General Dreedle and Colonel Cathcart). When the full horror becomes clear, as it is in this chapter, we are forced to reassess our former attitude. We are exposed to the gory, painful details of Snowden's demise and forced to remember that war is not funny, and should not be taken lightly. Also this encounter with death at its most visceral level gives Yossarian an insight into the nature of humanity, and the fact that human beings are merely 'matter:' vulnerable and mutable. He was helpless to save Snowden, or even to alleviate his suffering because Milo had stolen the ampoules of morphine for the benefit of his business; in their place he'd left a note saying, 'What's good for M&M Enterprises is good for the country.' This sounds very much like the language used to justify the disproportionate sacrifices that the men are making for the war effort—just as Cathcart defends increasing the missions with hollow patriotic clichés, so Milo's rhetoric is empty; both use the language of duty and sacrifice merely to further their own objectives.

By the time we get to the final chapter Yossarian has decided that he will not make a deal with Cathcart and Korn after all. He explains his position in a conversation with Major Danby. Danby is described as 'a gentle, moral, middle-aged idealist,' and though he tries to talk Yossarian out of it, it is clear that he admires his moral courage. There doesn't seem to be anywhere for him to turn at this stage: Cathcart and Korn have the power to court-martial and disgrace him, and he can no longer turn to Milo or ex-P.F.C. Wintergreen for help either. Whilst formerly antagonistic to one another in their various schemes and endeavours, these two have now become partners, and are reconciled, not only to each other, but to Colonel Cathcart also. The merger of Milo and Wintergreen is seen as a negative thing in the book because now M&M Enterprises has no competition, and the threat of monopoly capitalism is a dark one indeed, given what we know of Milo's blind, maniacal adherence to the creed of accumulation and profit. Just as Yossarian's position looks hopeless, however, the chaplain bursts onto the ward and tells him that Orr is alive in Sweden, where he appears to have been washed ashore following his crash. It seems that he had been planning his escape all along, and that his frequent accidents and landings on water were a deliberate preparation for his desertion. Inspired by Orr, Yossarian decides to desert also. As he bolts from the hospital Nately's whore is there to take another stab at him, but he evades her and flees into an uncertain future.

So Yossarian effectively opts out of the system, but this is not a cop-out. He could have lived comfortably within the system if he'd taken Cathcart and Korn's offer; instead he chooses a life on the run, refusing to compromise his new found moral consciousness. In other words, though Yossarian is apparently trying to escape at the end, this need not be seen as an escap*ist* ending. Many readers seem to assume that the hero is fleeing to join Orr at the end, a view reinforced by the film version of *Catch-22* (1970) where the closing scenes show Yossarian heading for Sweden in a boat. However, as Heller said in an interview with Charlie Reilly:

> Yossarian is running into danger, not away from it. He says there's a little girl in Rome whom he might be able to save. It's ironic that, after all the discussion about the ending of the novel, the film depicts Yossarian trying to row to Sweden. Nothing could have been farther from the case in the novel.[1]

Yossarian's so-called desertion is an act of bravery and, in a manner of speaking, his fight has just begun.

---

[1] Charlie Reilly, 'An Interview with Joseph Heller.' *Contemporary Literature*, Vol. 39, No. 4 (Winter, 1998), pp. 507–522.

# 5. Interpreting *Catch-22*

*Catch-22* has attracted a large body of scholarly work in the years since its publication—there are several book length studies focusing on Heller, and some that specifically address *Catch-22* itself. In addition there are countless critical articles that examine the book from every imaginable perspective. Here I will discuss a few of the common approaches to the novel, and assess what might be considered some of the key readings of Heller's book.

## 5.1. Yossarian as Individualist Hero

It is important that Yossarian does not accept Cathcart's and Korn's offer at the end of *Catch-22* because that would mean him yielding to the system, and would be difficult to square with his individualism. The latter is a significant aspect of his character, and key to how many have interpreted the novel. Heller himself wanted us to think of Yossarian as noble individual, with the courage of his convictions. In one interview he says that he had the hero Homer's *Iliad* in mind when he wrote the book:

> The *Iliad's* very first line talks about 'the dreadful anger of Achilles'—not about the fall of Troy or the Trojan horse or anything else. And the final scene with Priam shows Achilles' nobler side overcoming that wrath. *Catch-22* went beyond that, of course; it was very much concerned with attitudes toward war, attitudes toward bureaucracy [...] There is another echo of the *Iliad* insofar as the hierarchy of power is concerned. At the beginning Homer makes it clear Achilles isn't interested in acquiring another concubine; he wants Agamemnon to return the priest's daughter. When Agamemnon returns the girl and then steals Briseis, Achilles finds himself powerless. He broods in

his tent until Patroclus is killed and then he finally takes action. Yossarian is faced with a similar problem. He is powerless until, after Nately's death, he is driven to break the chain (Charlie Reilly, 'An Interview with Joseph Heller,' 518/9).

Like Achilles, Yossarian shows an honourable side at the end of *Catch-22*, and like him he decides to take action. Up till this point Yossarian has been largely reacting to his world; despite his irreverence and episodes of dissent, he has essentially accepted his lot. The death of his friend Nately causes him to 'break the chain' and become an *active* individual, asserting his right to autonomy, and striving to influence rather than be directed by events. So Yossarian can be seen as an individualist hero: someone who ultimately chooses to live life on his own terms, adhering to his own sense of what is right and wrong; and his decision not to compromise his convictions at the end can be viewed as honourable. As Yossarian's sense of morality cannot be reconciled with his corrupt environment, his only option—if he is to sustain his moral integrity—is to seek a way out.

Such individualist heroes are common in American narratives, and Yossarian is part of a tradition that extends back to early examples of American writing. The eponymous hero of Mark Twain's *Huckleberry Finn*, for instance, has a similar problem to Yossarian: he is at odds with his social world, and reluctant to be a part of it. Like Yossarian he rebels in various ways, and like Yossarian his rebellion continues beyond the close of the story. To have Huck assimilated into society at the end would be to undermine the spirit of individualism that is so fundamental to his character. So Huck flees to the frontier at the end of the story because this is an unsocialised space, free of the constraints of civilisation which he deems hypocritical and oppressive. Numerous critics have argued that this type of conflict is a recurring motif in American literature. Tony Tanner in *City of Words* (1970), for instance, sees it as a clash between innocence and experience: the innocence of the individualist hero conflicts with the experience forced upon him by society. Tanner writes that at the end of *Catch-22* Heller has

> Re-activated that most basic of American themes, the confrontation of innocence and experience. And as so often, the word

of experience is seen to be so unmitigatedly horrifying that the innocent hero cannot assimilate the experience, he can only flee from it.[1]

The world of experience is the world of corruption and injustice for Yossarian, just as it is for other American heroes like Huckleberry Finn; in order to retain his self-reliance and pursue his ideals he must escape the system: this is, Tanner suggests, 'the primordial gesture of the American hero,' vital for sustaining his individualism (*City of Words*, 79).

In a manner of speaking, there are lots of individualists in *Catch-22*. Characters like Colonel Cathcart, for instance, seek to promote their own interests, regardless of the consequences for others; and so does Milo, despite his claims to be working on everyone else's behalf: after all it is Milo, and only Milo, who is made mayor and worshipped as a god! Obviously there is a distinction to be made between this kind of selfishness and ruthless self-advancement, and Yossarian's brand of individualism. David Simmons suggests that the latter should be seen as an example of positive individualism, akin to the 'individualism of precapitalist America,' while the ruthless, selfish behaviour of characters like Milo reflects the 'negative individualism of capitalism.'[2] The precapitalist individualism that Simmons mentions is similar to the individualism of the classic frontier hero, like the figure of the cowboy, who has sense of morality that is innate rather than socially derived. This is the 'innocent,' as opposed to the 'experienced' individualism mentioned above. As the popularity of Westerns suggests, this innocent individualism is fondly regarded in American culture. The fact that Yossarian is a typical innocent individualist may partly account for the popularity of the novel in America. Yossarian is the quintessential nonconformist, even his nickname, Yo-Yo, refers to his unwillingness to fly in formation and obey those who threaten his interests. However, as suggested, the system he opposes is corrupt, so his is a benign, positive individual-

---

[1] Tony Tanner, *City of Words: American Fiction 1950-1970* (London: Jonathan Cape, 1971) 78
[2] David Simmons, *The Anti-Hero in the American Novel: From Joseph Heller to Kurt Vonnegut.* (New York: Palgrave Macmillan, 2008) 46–49

ism with a crucial moral facet. Certainly this is how he is interpreted by many critics.

In some ways Yossarian's so-called positive individualism is similar to that of a character like Sergeant Bilko of the *Phil Silvers Show*. This was a hugely popular American sitcom in the 50s and 60s, which also has a military theme. Like Bilko, Yossarian is a rebel, perhaps even a rogue, but like him he also cares about the other enlisted men and, ultimately, knows the difference between right and wrong. Another parallel might be Hawkeye Pierce, from the highly successful sitcom, M*A*S*H, set in the Korean War, which was based on Richard Hooker's 1968 novel, and ran through the 1970s. Hawkeye, a wise-cracking military doctor, is a character with similar traits, his dark humour combining with a highly sensitive nature. Hooker's novel, also filmed by Robert Altman, was inspired by *Catch-22*, and is another indication of how culturally significant the book has been.

It is hard not to conclude that the double-edged nature of Yossarian's character—his positive individualism—has contributed to his enduring appeal, particularly perhaps within modern capitalist society where individualism is encouraged, on the one hand, but only deemed acceptable when accompanied by a humanitarian concern on the other.

**5.2. Yossarian and Contemporary America**

While the novel is set in WWII, most critics see it as addressing modern America and what many considered the peculiar nature of post-War American life. As suggested earlier, it could be said that *Catch-22* turns to absurd humour in order to reflect a society that often appeared irrational and ridiculous; for some people, war provides a pertinent metaphor for the turbulent nature of post-War America. War is crazy, but modern American life seems just as bad; undoubtedly Heller himself felt that this was the principal focus of his satire in the book:

> Virtually none of the attitudes in the book—the suspicion and distrust of officials in government, the feelings of helplessness and victimisation, the realisation that most government agencies would lie—coincided with my experiences as a bombardier in

WWII. The anti-war and anti-government feelings in the book belong to the period following WWII: The Korean War, the Cold War of the Fifties. A general disintegration of belief took place then, and it affected *Catch-22*.[1]

Many critics have observed a parallel between Yossarian's world and that of the Cold War and the McCarthy era. For instance, Tony Hilfer points out that Captains Black's elaborate loyalty oaths parody the behaviour of the House Committee on Un-American Activities. This was the Committee whose job it was to investigate alleged threats of subversion or attempts to undermine America's interests during the extremely sensitive Cold War period. At Committee hearings people were interrogated about their links to the Communist party, with interrogators looking for ways of exposing suspects as disloyal to the States. The Kafkaesque interrogation of the chaplain in *Catch-22* can be read in exactly this way:

> 'I have here another affidavit from Colonel Cathcart that states that you once told him that atheism was not against the law. Do you recall ever making that statement to anyone?'
> The Chaplain nodded without hesitation, feeling himself on very solid ground now. 'Yes sir, I did make a statement like that. I made it because it's true. Atheism is not against the law.'
> 'But that's still no reason to say so, Chaplain, is it?' the officer chided tartly (*Catch-22*, 407/8).

As Hilfer suggests, 'The comic technique is *reduction ad absurdum* yet it is not far from conventional political logic;'[2] and the intention is for it to mirror the logic applied by some of the inquisitors during the Un-American Activities investigations: it is merely a matter of substituting the word atheism with un-American.

The Vietnam War became a parallel for Heller's story post-publication, of course, and that fact that this conflict raged throughout the 60s made *Catch-22* seem highly relevant. Certainly as the decade moved on and the war intensified, it is hard not to imagine that it was this, rather than WWII, that was in most people's thoughts as they

---
1 Joseph Heller, 'Reeling in Catch 22.' In *Catch as Catch Can: The Collected Stories and Other Writings.*' (London: Simon and Schuster, 2003) 314.
2 Tony Hilfer, *American Fiction Since 1940* (London: Longman, 1992) 114

accompanied Yossarian through his nightmare:

> *Catch-22* answered most to an audience that saw the novel's structural logic as a perfect reflection of the American engagement in Vietnam. The rhetoric of body counts, the proclamation of a general who claimed that he had destroyed a Vietnamese city in order to save it—this and other aspects of Vietnam seemed a Heller invention, and extension of the logic of *Catch-22* (Tony Hilfer, *American Fiction Since 1940*, 115–6).

Despite its status as a WWII story, then, and despite the fact that it was mostly written in the 1950s, the novel remained strikingly apposite to the times after publication; and in this respect too it has affinities with M*A*S*H which, though set during the Korean War, clearly offered a parallel for Vietnam. Sadly, similar conflicts remain a part of our lives, as does the rhetoric of governments who attempt to justify them, and this might go some way toward explaining why *Catch-22* continues to be read and discussed so widely.

## 5.3. Yossarian as Mythic Hero

It has been mentioned that the novel was inspired partly by the *Iliad*, and a number of critics offer readings of *Catch-22* that stress its affinities with this and other mythical tales. Jon Woodson, for instance, in *A Study of Joseph Heller's Catch-22: Going around Twice*, argues that the myth criticism Heller studied as a postgraduate student influenced his themes in the novel: he follows writers like T. S. Eliot in employing a mythical substructure for his work, basing the story heavily on the Sumerian epic *Gilgamesh*, generally considered to be the world's oldest tale.[1] Similarly David M. Craig argues that Yossarian has a strong mythical dimension, particularly regarding the hero's attempts to cheat death—to 'live forever or die in the attempt.' He too sees affinities with *Gilgamesh*, together with the Bible, and, chiefly, with the tale of Prometheus. Prometheus in the Greek myth steals fire from the god Zeus in order to give it to mortal man, thereby becoming a kind of champion of humanity, and

---

[1] Jon Woodson, *A Study of Joseph Heller's Catch-22: Going around Twice* (New York, NY: Peter Lang, 2001)

this is how Craig interprets Yossarian.

As an example of this kind of approach to *Catch-22*, it is worth looking at David Craig's critique in more depth. He suggests that the parallels between Yossarian and Prometheus are reinforced partly by the novel's abundant references to liver. In the myth of Prometheus, Zeus punishes him for the crime of stealing fire by binding him to a rock at the mercy of an eagle which eats his liver day after day: each day his liver grows back, the eagle eats it again. Heller includes many mentions of liver in *Catch-22*—there is Yossarian's claim to suffer from a liver problem, for instance, and Captain Black's cruel delight in forcing people to 'eat' their livers.' We get to see Snowden's liver when his death is described, of course, and at one stage Yossarian faces the threat of a liver operation. According to Craig, these references are so abundant that, 'By the novel's end, Yossarian's liver problem has become a Promethean malady.'[1]

Craig contends that Yossarian's attempts to evade death have a mythical facet insofar as 'Yossarian echoes Prometheus's cry of defiance to Zeus, "my mind remains immortal and unsubdued"' (Craig, *Tilting at Mortality*, 50). Yossarian, like Prometheus, challenges the supreme authority of God, and his course through the story becomes a journey of maturation, a passage from ignorance to insight. All through the novel Yossarian is shown to be preoccupied with his own mortality—not just in terms of the war, and the possibility of being killed in action, but also in relation to his physical health. Certainly Heller underscores the point that Yossarian is scared of dying. In order to cheat death, however, he must, like Prometheus, become acquainted with his inner self. Craig argues that this is exactly what happens, and Yossarian's story can be seen as an initiation narrative, charting a period in which he acquires knowledge, to a point where he learns how to use that knowledge to achieve self-understanding.

Craig unravels the disrupted chronology of the story and argues that Yossarian begins in state of innocence in the hospital: 'the earliest episode occurs at the hospital at Lowery Field where, thanks to a sympathetic doctor, Yossarian discovers the power of his liver ail-

---

[1] David M. Craig, *Tilting at Mortality: Narrative Strategies in Joseph Heller's Fiction* (Detroit: Wayne State University Press, 1997) 51

ment' (Craig, *Tilting at Mortality,* 52). In hospital he can escape the war and feel safe, but he also acquires knowledge: an understanding of how death can be thwarted, in this case by exaggerating the severity of his ailment. In hospital Yossarian experiences a kind of symbolic death when he impersonates Giuseppe, the soldier who dies before his family had a chance to say goodbye. Yossarian's innocent self perishes when he hears Giuseppe's father make the point that it is not right for young people to die. From now on, according to Craig, just as Prometheus resists Zeus in order to save humans from death, so Yossarian is on a similar mission. Now death is Yossarian's enemy; he is no longer ignorant and naïve, he has knowledge that will enable him to defy death, and a task, which is: 'to save humans from death by teaching them how to live.'

Yossarian emerges from the hospital reborn as a wiser man, then, and he is now ready for phase two of his initiation, which takes place on his bombing missions. These missions deepen his understanding of death—in other words they give him more of an insight into his enemy. They culminate with the Avignon mission and the death of Snowden. As we know, Heller leaves it till the end of the novel before he reveals this in all its gruesome detail. When eventually it is shown we see that Yossarian reads a message in Snowden's entrails.

> It was easy to read the message [...] man was matter. That was Snowden's secret. Drop him out a window and he'll fall. Set fire to him and he'll burn. Bury him and he'll rot like other kinds of garbage. The spirit gone, man is garbage. That was Snowden's secret. Ripeness was all (Quoted in Craig, *Tilting at Mortality,* 59)

If 'Ripeness was all,' then the only thing worth having is life; in other words, here Yossarian achieves deeper self-knowledge—that without life he is 'garbage.' Having achieved this insight he can refocus: 'with his hard-won knowledge, Yossarian shifts his attention from death to life' (Craig, *Tilting at Mortality,* 59), and eventually he comes to understand that, 'in order to live he must abandon public duty and dedicate himself to personal survival' (Craig, *Tilting at Mortality,* 53). This does not mean aligning himself with Colonels Cathcart and Korn, which would itself be another form of death: the death of Yossarian's individualism. Rather, he embraces the latter, refusing to compromise his sense of right and wrong, refusing to become part of the system that continues to oppress and destroy the men. With his self-knowledge and self-respect intact, he opts out of the system, and the war. According to Craig this has affinities with the 'Promethean legacy' expressed in the mythical hero's statement: 'I caused men to no longer foresee their death;' in a similar way, Yossarian's insight teaches him and us not to dwell on death: this refocusing is life-affirming, and shows us the way to cheat death in life.

**5.4. Yossarian as Postmodern Hero.**

Most scholars would agree that *Catch-22* has affinities with postmodernist writing. The term postmodernism is not easy to define, but in literature it's generally used to refer to writing that emerged after WWII, and which is playful, sceptical, and ironic about its ability to express truth in narrative. Without actually using the term, Heller himself referred to this phenomenon as a 'general disintegration of belief' that manifested itself in his work, and that of other writers after the War:

> Without being aware of it, I was part of a near-movement in fiction. While I was writing *Catch-22*, J. P. Donleavy was writing *The Ginger Man*, Jack Kerouac was writing *On the Road*, Ken Kesey was writing *One Flew Over the Cuckoo's Nest*, Thomas Pynchon was writing *V.*, and Kurt Vonnegut was writing *Cat's Cradle*. I don't think any one of us even knew any of the others. Certainly I didn't know them. Whatever forces were at work shaping a trend in art were affecting not just me, but all of us (Heller, 'Reeling in *Catch-22*,' *Catch as Catch Can*, 314).

Writers associated with postmodernism are suspicious of certainty, particularly in relation to notions of value: they tend to dispute the idea that there are fixed criteria for evaluating questions of ethics, aesthetics and politics. They are wary of narratives that construct themselves as authorities—that is which purport to offer the truth—partly because of their sense of the limitations of language. Increasingly in the mid-to-late-twentieth century, theorists began to stress that language is an abstract system of signs with no fixed relationship with the world it seeks to describe, and the implications of this became significant for many writers and thinkers. For instance, how can language be said to represent reality when its meanings are arbitrary and constantly in flux? There is always going to be a mismatch between reality and attempts to describe it. This mismatch between language and reality is a major theme for many postmodern writers, and it is central to *Catch-22*.

One of the first scholars to address this aspect of Heller's book is Gary W. Davis. He points out that there is a discontinuity between language and reality in the novel which manifests itself in a variety of ways. For instance, 'names, in *Catch-22*, often fail to "properly" designate a particular object, person, or concept;'[1] words do not mean what they are supposed to. At the outset Yossarian is seen transforming meaning at will as he censors the men's letters; Caleb Major finds that he is no longer who he thought he was after being assigned the identity of a stranger, Major Major Major. Examples of this kind of thing pervade the novel, and augment our sense of the gap between the word and the world. The Army takes advantage of this, together with the way language can influence meaning and create its own reality. For instance, the phrase 'bomb patterns' becomes a key feature of Air Corps policy, despite the fact that, as General Peckham admits, it means nothing. As Davis suggests:

> The Army's entire administrative procedure arises from this ability to put purposeless, self-reflexive discourse into action within its field of activity. Ultimately its self-contained organization and action define a closed world whose 'illusory depth' becomes its inhabitants' only 'reality' (Davis '*Catch-22* and the Language of Discontinuity,' 70).

Things which appear to have meaning, which appear to make sense, do not. This is crucial to Yossarian's predicament as he tries to locate himself in a world where language cannot be reconciled with common sense. The principal example is the illogical-logic of Catch-22 itself, which illustrates, 'how signifiers, psychological definitions, and knowledge itself are deployed without reference to any "real"

---

[1] Gary W. Davis '*Catch-22* and the Language of Discontinuity.' *Novel: A Forum on Fiction*, Vol. 12, No. 1 (Autumn, 1978), pp. 66–77 (68)

human or natural content.' Davis discusses how this relates to the issue of Orr's sanity:

> The 'elliptical precision' of this logic [of Catch-22] reveals that the word 'crazy' and the question of Orr's sanity are relevant only to whether he flies combat missions or asks to be grounded. Since both actions are functions of the Army's discontinuous rules, sanity and selfhood are now revealed to be elements of a field of play which is as closed as Yossarian's games with the soldiers' letters. Moreover, by showing that Orr's sanity is to be determined solely on the basis of whether he does or does not agree to fly more missions, Catch-22 demands that we think of the self as unrelated moments of discourse rather than as a continuous or creative entity in itself (Davis, 'Catch-22 and the Language of Discontinuity,' 70).

Just like language, the system that governs Yossarian's world is abstract and arbitrary, cut off from reality. It has its own internal logic, which does not correspond to what we might call real world logic; however, because the characters are trapped within the system, this system-defined logic is the only logic available. It effectively allows the Army to construct meaning, as when the living and breathing Doc Daneeka is constructed as deceased, or the law-abiding chaplain is constructed as a villain, or when Yossarian is constructed as a dying Italian soldier who has already died. This phenomenon features too in the deeds of Milo Minderbinder:

> Milo's power is based upon two general assumptions: that everyone agrees to and has a 'share' in his syndicate, and that there is, beneath this, some 'proper' relation between the shares and a 'reality' beyond. These assumptions help Milo create a mercantile empire which, like the capitalist system itself, holds a controlling interest in many of the combatant armies. The very essence of Milo's endeavour, though, exists solely as discourse. The shares are only the words 'A Share' written on the nearest scrap of paper' and the syndicate's profits always are as fictional as its shares (Davis, 'Catch-22 and the Language of Discontinuity,' 72).

Again like language, and like the system of meaning that operates within the Army, the function of Milo's system depends on the assumption that his symbols correspond to reality, that they have meaning. Of course they do not: they are merely scraps of paper.

It seems that the only escape for Yossarian is to flee the system that controls meaning, and this is exactly what he longs to do, particularly in his dream of following Orr's flight to Sweden. The issue is whether this could ever constitute a *genuine* escape. It could be argued that as a postmodern novel, *Catch-22* is underpinned by the premise that what is true of the system within the army, counts for the world in general. The mismatch between language and reality that is everywhere in Yossarian's life as a soldier, is everywhere in life generally. As Davis points out, the image he has of Sweden—as a benign environment of freedom—is also the product of a system that distorts reality:

> Yossarian's vision of Sweden [is] as a place of even more than political refuge and physical safety, a land, he thinks, where 'the girls are so sweet' and the 'people are so advanced.' It is a place whose image as a kind of regained paradise reveals that its bases are, like those of *Catch-22* itself, founded on the myths of natural experience and a 'proper' metaphoric language as the foundation of value (Davis, '*Catch-22* and the Language of Discontinuity,' 75).

Yossarian dreams of Sweden are fictional because, in a manner of speaking, this is all that words can create: a perversion of reality that, like the perversions of reality he experiences from day to day in the army, has similar potential to frustrate. Ultimately Yossarian's desire for freedom can never be satisfied, then, because there is no context in which he can achieve it: the distorting systems are everywhere. This type of reading positions Yossarian as a postmodernist hero in an 'unending struggle to discover and free [his] own being' (Davis, '*Catch-22* and the Language of Discontinuity,' 77); and, because that struggle is 'unending,' it is futile.

### 5.5. Yossarian as the Hero of a Bad Novel

As suggested, not all reviews of Heller's book were positive when it was published in 1961, and over the years it has attracted some negative responses from scholars who dispute its status as a masterpiece. Though most acknowledge that it is an important book, not all academics agree that it has the makings of an enduring classic. Richard Lehan and Jerry Patch, for instance, claim that the novel is 'inchoate and inconclusive, cracking in places under its own weight.' Whilst admitting that it has some merits, they claim that the more ludicrous elements in the story are a major aesthetic flaw. Sections such as the one where Milo organises a bombing mission on his own base, for instance, border on silliness, and it is hard to give credence to them; they argue that Heller 'heavy-handedly destroyed the underlying truth by allowing them to become mere farce.'[1] Norman Podhoretz also criticises the novel for aesthetic reasons, but he attacks it on moral grounds too, arguing that *Catch-22*

> justified draft evasion and even desertion as morally superior to military service. After all, if the hero of *Catch-22*, fighting in the best of all possible wars, was right to desert and run off to Sweden [...] How much more justified were his Vietnam-era disciples in following the trail he so prophetically blazed.[2]

So this critic feels that it is morally unsound because it encourages draft-dodging.

It is perhaps no coincidence that both of these unfavourable critiques feature in books on *Catch-22* edited by Harold Bloom: the first in his *Modern Critical Interpretations* series, the second in his *Bloom's Guides* series. Bloom is a highly respected, internationally renowned critic—Sterling Professor of Humanities at Yale University—but he is also someone who feels that Heller's novel has been overpraised. In one introduction he consigns '*Catch-22* to the vast heap of Period Pieces;' and argues that

> it is not a masterpiece, but a tendentious burlesque, founded upon a peculiarly subjective view of historical reality. Subjectivity,

---

[1] Richard Lehan and Jerry Patch. '*Catch-22*: The Making of a New Novel.' In Harold Bloom, ed., *Bloom's Modern Critical Interpretations: Joseph Heller's Catch-22* (New York: Bloom's Literary Criticism An imprint of Infobase Publishing, 2008) 81–91 (82)

[2] Norman Podhoretz. 'Looking Back at *Catch-22*' in Harold Bloom, ed., *Bloom's Guides: Joseph Heller's Catch-22* (New York: Bloom's Literary Criticism An imprint of Infobase Publishing, 2009) 223–233 (229)

to be persuasive, requires lucidity, and nothing in *Catch-22* is lucid.[1]

Bloom claims that it is of temporary value partly because it is a comic novel that functions mainly at the level of satire and parody—such comic genres are inevitably ephemeral because they are culturally specific, dependent on a historical moment, and once that moment has gone so has the force of the humour; for Bloom *Catch-22* 'no longer induces either laughter or shock.' Of course this is the danger with all comedy, and that is why it is occasionally treated as an inferior genre to tragedy by scholars. According to this view it is hard for comedies to achieve the status of classics—comedy is often trivial and fleeting, and for a novel to become a classic it must by definition possess qualities that transcend its historical and cultural circumstances. Also, as far as Bloom is concerned, some of the humour in Heller's book simply does not work; like Lehan and Patch, he feels that some episodes are too silly, and this diminishes the whole: 'Madness is mocked by *Catch-22*, but the mockery loses control and enters the space of literary irreality, where only a few masters have been able to survive. Heller was not one of them.' Again, the accusation is that Heller's humour becomes excessive, implausible, and inappropriate. As with Podhoretz, Bloom also disapproves of the book on moral grounds; like him, he is particularly critical of the ending:

> Yossarian's war ends with his departure for Sweden, a desertion that Heller presents as a triumph, which it has to be, if the war as aptly characterized by Heller's parodistic cast of con-men, schemers, profiteers, and mad commanders. War is obscene, necessarily, but the war against Hitler, the SS, and the death camps was neither World War I nor the Vietnam debacle. Heller isolates the reader from the historical reality of Hitler's evil, yet nevertheless the war against the Nazis was also Yossarian's war. (Harold Bloom. 'Introduction,' *Bloom's Modern Critical Interpretations: Joseph Heller's Catch-22)* 1-2.

Yossarian's flight at the end of the book is morally dubious in Bloom's view—he asks whether, if we are meant to view the ending in positive

---
1 Harold Bloom, 'Introduction,' In Harold Bloom ed., *Bloom's Modern Critical Interpretations: Joseph Heller's Catch-22* (1–2).

terms, we are to assume that Hitler should have gone unopposed? Unlike the Vietnam War, WWII was a morally justifiable, necessary war, and desertion, particularly one that is celebrated as a legitimate escape, must be considered a potentially irresponsible, and perhaps even immoral act. Of course such readings fail to take into account that Yossarian has actually done his fair share of fighting before he deserts. His desertion is largely a response to Cathcart's decision continually to raise the number of missions that the men have to fly, which itself could be considered a morally unsound action. Most would probably agree that this mitigates Yossarian's desertion. It is certainly true that Heller does, as Bloom suggests, isolate the reader from 'the historical reality of Hitler's evil,' but as numerous critics, and Heller himself have argued, *Catch-22* is not about Hitler, but about modern America, so it is arguably not appropriate to judge the book in terms of its fidelity to the facts, or the lived experience of the conflict.

**5.6. Yossarian as an Old Man: Closing Time**

In 1994 Heller published a sequel to *Catch-22*, *Closing Time*. As his biographer says, 'many reviewers suggested the sequel dimmed the reputation of *Catch-22* and tarnished Joe's career' (Tracy Daugherty, *Just One Catch*, 438), but nevertheless the novel is important in the degree to which it might help us understand *Catch-22*, and Heller's attitude to its themes as an older man.

*Closing Time* is set in late twentieth century New York, with Yossarian in his 70s. He now works for Milo Minderbinder, who has become a globally successful entrepreneur and arms dealer. Yossarian is commissioned to organise a wedding for Milo's son, M2, in New York's Port Authority Bus Terminal, and the multi-million dollar spectacle of this event constitutes part of the novel's climax. Alongside this Heller tells the stories of two other WWII veterans: Lew Rabinowitz and Sammy Singer. The former is dying of Hodgkin's disease and the latter, having lost his wife, is due to embark on a round the world trip during which he hopes to find meaning at the end of his life. The book offers substantial back stories for Lew and Sammy, including details of their friendship, their war experiences, and how they relate to Yossarian's in *Catch 22*. Many of the characters from the former novel are referred to, as are several characters from the history of fiction, such as Ashenbach, hero of Thomas Mann's *Death in Venice*, and Schviek from Hašek's *The Good Soldier*. Lew and Sammy's various war reminiscences also include references to real-life writers such as Kurt Vonnegut, and to Heller himself who appears as 'Joey Heller.' This gives the book a rather self-conscious, metafictional feel that Heller has employed before in novels such as *Good as Gold*. Metafiction is often a feature of postmodern writing, employed to problematize the relationship between fiction and reality, and it might be that Heller uses it here to draw our attention to the fact that his novels and his life are related.

Alongside Milo Minderbinder, another key character to reappear is the chaplain. He remains a hapless individual who finds himself the subject of unwanted government attention when he begins to urinate heavy water, a component used in the production of atomic weapons. The prospect of nuclear war becomes a feature of the plot, and the book ends with the inept U.S. President—known only as the Little Prick—triggering a nuclear strike, and potentially the end of the world. The wealthy capitalist élite seek sanctuary in a bunker miles below the Port Authority Bus Terminal, but Yossarian—though he has the option to join them—chooses to take his chances above ground with his pregnant young girlfriend, a nurse he met in whilst in hospital. The end of Yossarian's story is offered alongside the end of Sammy Singer's, who we last see on a plane bound for Australia, alone in the world after the death of his wife, and his old friend Lew. In an interview with Ramona Kovel conducted shortly before his death, Heller discusses the ending:

> There are two endings to the book just as largely two novels in that one book. One is the typically romantic, happy, unrealistic fictional ending in which the character is coming up from safety into a world that maybe under attack to keep a date with a woman he loves, I think I describe the unrealistic belief that they would live happily for ever after. And then the other ending is with the realistic figure called Sammy Singer who is largely

> based on my own life [...] flying to Australia on a vacation, his wife has died, he's desperately lonely, and he knows his life is going to be coming to an end.[1]

The aim was to contrast Yossarian's optimism with Sammy's fatalism: where Sammy is reconciled to the prospect of death, Yossarian, as in *Catch 22*, battles against a world that seems intent on dictating his future.

Many critics identified major problems with both plots. For one thing Yossarian has become something of an insider, wealthy and comfortable, and reconciled to the kind of system he formerly rebelled against. This is particularly evident in his association with Milo, a character who he admits to liking despite his obvious shortcomings. This undermines our sense of Yossarian as a principled individualist: in other words the trait that enabled us to emotionally engage with him. Also, of course, no one is trying to kill him, a major source of dramatic tension in the first novel that is missing here. As for the parallel plot, the author spends a disproportionate amount of time detailing the lives of Lew and Sammy, and their stories lack energy and suspense. Their war recollections are protracted and directionless, and as such are devoid of the kind of suspense necessary to drive a story. Indeed, their war reminiscences often involve retelling key episodes from *Catch 22*, which creates feelings of déjà vu, but rarely offers fresh or interesting perspectives on these familiar scenes. As Scott Bradfield said in his review of the book, 'Because *Closing Time* can generate no comic momentum of its own, characters are always recollecting, in very stilted dialogue, major highlights from *Catch-22*.'[2] Such recollections lack the immediacy and the absurdist comic energy of Heller's masterpiece. While there a few moments of successful humour—largely confined to Yossarian's dialogues which occasionally employ funny reversals of logic akin to the absurdist comedy of *Catch 22*—the book doesn't work well as a novel. At one stage Yossarian recommends Thomas Mann's *Death in Venice* to his

---

1 'Ramona Koval in conversation with American novelist and memoirist Joseph Heller.' *Books and Writing*, 1999. See bibliography for web address.
2 Scott Bradfield, 'Yossarian the insider dealer: *Closing Time.' The Independent* Saturday, 1 October 1994. See bibliography for web address.

son Michael and then reflects on what the hero Aschenbach's story means to him; his reflections could be read as Heller's comment on his own sequel:

> Aschenbach too had run out of interests, although he distracted himself with his ridiculous obsession and the conceit that there was still much left for him to do. He was an artist of the intellect who had tired of working on projects that would no longer yield to even his most patient effort, and he knew he was faking it. But he did not know that his creative life was over and that he and his era were coming to a close.[1]

We can only speculate as to whether Heller identifies with Aschenbach's inability to make his art 'yield' at this point in his life, but it's hard not to see this problem as being relevant to *Closing Time*, and the author's failure to make it cohere. Did Heller feel that his creative life was over, and that his sequel was proof of that fact?

Despite its shortcomings, the book is interesting for fans of *Catch 22*, because it offers an insight into Heller's attitude to his characters in later life, and this is particularly relevant in the case of Yossarian. Heller was a self-confessed sceptic and Yossarian mostly shares this doubting tendency. The problem with being a sceptic is that it can make it difficult to form opinions and, as Yossarian tells his son Michael at one point, 'A problem I have […] is that I'm almost always able to see both sides of every question' (Joseph Heller, *Closing Time*, 189). Such a position can be equated with a lack of values and an inability to make commitments; indeed, it could be argued that for much of *Catch 22* Yossarian's only real commitment is to his own survival. This changes at the end, as we have seen, and in the sequel Heller takes this a stage further, reminding us again of the value of conviction. At the end of *Closing Time* he elects to take his chance with the young woman he's fallen in love with, choosing a precarious and probably fleeting life above ground with her, as opposed to survival below ground. While this may be foolish, we are meant to applaud Yossarian's optimism and his willingness to commit. At the end of his life, Heller himself comes to feel that such an outlook is preferable to scepticism, and the most likely route to happiness, as he says

---

1  Joseph Heller, *Closing Time* (New York: Simon and Schuster, 1994) 242–3.

in interview with Koval:

> I have to acknowledge even though I myself can't have beliefs, unquestioning beliefs in anything, I do recognise that I would be better off if I did ('Ramona Koval in Conversation with Joseph Heller').

It is worth noting, then, that Heller wanted to imbue his most famous comic creation with traits that he himself lacked—faith and optimism. In so doing he aligns Yossarian with some of the most prominent characters in twentieth century American writing, such as Jay Gatsby and Willy Loman—the former is the hero of Scott Fitzgerald's novel *The Great Gatsby* (1925), and the latter of Arthur Miller's play *Death of a Salesman* (1945). Both characters have faith in a misguided ideal—versions of the American Dream—and possess faith and optimism that, in one sense at least, fails to lead anywhere positive. Similarly, we can't help but feel that Yossarian may have become something of a doomed dreamer. While Yossarian feels 'in his gut' that he, his girlfriend, and their baby 'would survive, flourish, and live happily-forever after,' it is his son, Michael's, perspective that seems the more realistic:

> As he saw Yossarian riding up away from him on the escalator to keep a lunch date with his pregnant girlfriend, Michael, who'd been both proud and embarrassed by his father's love affair, had the listless, desolate feeling that one of them was dying, maybe both (Joseph Heller, *Closing Time*, 461).

Having said this, the idea of Yossarian risking his life for an unlikely future with a younger woman has some appeal, in the same way that Gatsby and Loman's belief and optimism appeals, despite its apparent futility. It may constitute self-deceit, but what some people call self-deceit, of course, other people call faith. Certainly his decision sustains our sense of his irrepressible spirit, and his willingness to battle against the odds. It is a fitting image with which to close Yossarian's story, and with which to end this discussion.

# 6. Bibliography

### 6.1. Other Relevant Books by Heller

Heller, Joseph., *Something Happened*, (New York: Knopf, 1974). This is the novel he published after *Catch-22*, which some consider to be his greatest literary achievement; certainly it is the book that students should seek out first if they are interested in reading his later fiction.

———. *Closing Time* (New York: Simon and Schuster, 1994). The much disparaged sequel to *Catch-22*. This book does not really work well as a novel in its own right, but it is of immense interest to students of Heller's classic. It is best read as a supplement to *Catch-22*, and it is useful for the insight it offers into the author's view of his characters' relevance to the modern world.

———. *Now and Then: A Memoir from Coney Island to Here*. (London: Simon & Schuster, 1998). Heller's autobiography largely sticks to the literal facts about his life, and does not reveal that much about his emotions or his relationships. It provides useful context for *Catch-22*, however, particularly in relation to Heller's war time experiences.

———. *Catch as Catch Can: The Collected Stories and Other Writings*. (London: Simon and Schuster, 2003). This very useful book collects together Heller's early fiction, together with various autobiographical pieces and interviews of relevance to *Catch-22*.

### 6.2. Catch-22 Film

*Catch-22*, director, Nichols, Mike., (Hollywood: Paramount, 2001). DVD. The film version of the novel, released in 1970, is available on DVD and stars Alan Arkin as Yossarian. Lovers of the book may find his rather nervy portrayal of the hero difficult to square with Heller's original. Heller himself appeared to think highly of the film, however, and the director certainly went to considerable lengths to make it realistic, including collecting together eighteen B-25 bombers, which at the time of filming was the twelfth largest air force in the world!

## 6.3. Books about Heller

Bloom, Harold, ed., *Bloom's Modern Critical Interpretations: Joseph Heller's Catch-22* (New York: Bloom's Literary Criticism An imprint of Infobase Publishing, 2008). This is one of the most recent collections of articles to focus on *Catch-22*. Among other things it contains an essay examining the parallels between Heller and Yossarian's war experiences, together with useful essays on structure and themes in the book. It also includes a piece on the sequel to *Catch-22, Closing Time*.

Daugherty, Tracy, *Just One Catch: A Biography of Joseph Heller* (New York: St. Martins Press, 2011). This first book-length biography of Joseph Heller is comprehensive and extremely readable. It is particularly useful for students who seek a deeper understanding of Heller; not surprisingly Daugherty spends a good portion of the book discussing the genesis of *Catch-22*.

Heller, Erica, *Yossarian Slept Here: When Joseph Heller was Dad and Life was a Catch-22* (London: Vintage, 2011). This is a memoir produced by Heller's daughter, offering a fascinating first-hand account of the author's life before and after the publication of his most famous novel. It provides an excellent supplement to Tracy Daugherty's biography.

Seed, David, *The Fiction of Joseph Heller: Against the Grain*, (New York: St. Martin's Press, 1989). A general book on Heller's fiction which makes a case for the quality and significance of Heller's other writing that is often overshadowed by *Catch-22*. Seed offers a detailed and intelligent reading of *Catch-22* too, and uses it as a reference point for his discussion of the later work.

Sorkin, Adam J., ed., *Conversations with Joseph Heller* (Jackson: University Press of Mississippi, 1993). This contains many of the important interviews with Heller up to the early nineties, including his long *The Paris Review* interview with George Plimpton, and notable celebrity interviews with the likes of Mel Brooks and Martin Amis.

### 6.4. Books on Modern American Writing

Hilfer, Tony., *American Fiction Since 1940.* (London: Longman, 1992). A valuable study of mid-to-late twentieth century American writing; it includes an excellent Chapter on *Catch-22*, together with a cogent analysis of *Something Happened.*

McDonald, Paul, *Laughing at the Darkness: Optimism and Postmodernism in American Humour* (Humanities E-Books. Approaches to Contemporary American Literature, 2011). This has a Chapter on Jewish American humour and WWII, and would be useful for anyone looking to follow up the points made in this guide about American literary postmodernism.

Simmons, David, *The Anti-Hero in the American Novel: From Joseph Heller to Kurt Vonnegut.* (New York: Palgrave Macmillan, 2008). A useful book for those seeking to develop a deeper understanding of mid-twentieth century American fiction, particularly in relation to the figure of the anti-hero; Simmons's study provides an accessible insight into the intellectual and aesthetic preoccupations that have a bearing on the development of *Catch-22*.

### 6.5. Online Material

Bradfield, Scott, 'Yossarian the Insider Dealer: *Closing Time.*' *The Independent* Saturday, 1 October 1994. This is a review of *Closing Time*, succinctly outlining what many critics agree are flaws in the novel.

http://www.independent.co.uk/arts-entertainment/books/book-review--yossarian-the-insider-dealer-closing-time--joseph-heller-simon--schuster-1499-pounds-joseph-heller-has-written-a-sequel-to-catch22-scott-bradfield-wonders-why-1440142.html

Koval, Ramona, 'In Conversation with American Novelist and Memoirist Joseph Heller.' This is a transcript of an interview with Heller conducted for the show *Books and Writing*, broadcast on Radio National in Australia in December 1999. It includes an excerpt from *Closing Time*, and a detailed discussion of this novel and its relationship to *Catch-22*.

http://www.abc.net.au/rn/arts/bwriting/stories/s97285.htm

Krassner, Paul, 'An Impolite Interview with Joseph Heller,' *The Realist*, #39, November 1962. This substantial early interview with Heller has been archived and is available to read for free. Here he talks at length about the origins of *Catch-22*.

http://www.ep.tc/realist/39/19.html

Guttridge, Peter, 'Joseph Heller: Obituary,' *The Independent*, Wednesday 15 December 1999. Heller's death prompted numerous obituaries in newspapers around the world. This one offers a concise, but thoughtful assessment of the author's career.

http://www.independent.co.uk/arts-entertainment/obituaries-joseph-heller-1132504.html

# A Note on the Author

Paul McDonald works at the University of Wolverhampton where he is Senior Lecturer in American Literature and Course Leader for Creative Writing. He is the author of eleven books, including three poetry collections and three comic novels.

His criticism includes books on Philip Roth, the fiction of the Industrial Midlands, and postmodern American Humour. His research focuses largely on comedy, and he takes a perverse pleasure in the fact that Googling 'the oldest joke in the world' generates several hundred pages with his name on.

# Humanities-Ebooks.co.uk

*All Humanities Ebooks titles are available to Libraries through EBSCO and MyiLibrary.com*

## Some Academic titles

Sibylle Baumbach, *Shakespeare and the Art of Physiognomy*
John Beer, *Blake's Humanism*
John Beer, *The Achievement of E M Forster*
John Beer, *Coleridge the Visionary*
Jared Curtis, ed., *The Fenwick Notes of William Wordsworth**
Jared Curtis, ed., *The Cornell Wordsworth: A Supplement**
Steven Duncan, *Analytic Philosophy of Religion: its History since 1955**
John K Hale, *Milton as Multilingual: Selected Essays 1982–2004*
Simon Hull, ed., *The British Periodical Text, 1797–1835*
Rob Johnson, Mark Levene and Penny Roberts, eds., *History at the End of the World **
John Lennard, *Modern Dragons and other Essays on Genre Fiction**
C W R D Moseley, *Shakespeare's History Plays*
Paul McDonald, *Laughing at the Darkness: Postmodernism and American Humour **
Colin Nicholson, *Fivefathers: Interviews with late Twentieth-Century Scottish Poets*
W J B Owen, *Understanding 'The Prelude'*
Pamela Perkins, ed., *Francis Jeffrey's Highland and Continental Tours**
Keith Sagar, *D. H. Lawrence: Poet**
Reinaldo Francisco Silva, *Portuguese American Literature**
William Wordsworth, *Concerning the Convention of Cintra**
W J B Owen and J W Smyser, eds., *Wordsworth's Political Writings**
*The Poems of William Wordsworth: Collected Reading Texts from the Cornell Wordsworth*, 3 vols.*

\* These titles are also available in print using links from
http://www.humanities-ebooks.co.uk

# Humanities Insights

These are some of the Insights available at:
http://www.humanities-ebooks.co.uk/

### General Titles

An Introduction to Critical Theory
Modern Feminist Theory
An Introduction to Rhetorical Terms

### Genre FictionSightlines

Octavia E Butler: *Xenogenesis / Lilith's Brood*
Reginal Hill: *On Beulah's Height*
Ian McDonald: *Chaga / Evolution's Store*
Walter Mosley: *Devil in a Blue Dress*
Tamora Pierce: *The Immortals*

### History Insights

Oliver Cromwell
The British Empire: Pomp, Power and Postcolonialism
The Holocaust: Events, Motives, Legacy
Lenin's Revolution
Methodism and Society
The Risorgimento

### Literature Insights

Austen: *Emma*
Conrad: *The Secret Agent*
Eliot, T S: 'The Love Song of J Alfred Prufrock' and *The Waste Land*
English Renaissance Drama: Theatre and Theatres in Shakespeare's Time
Reading William Faulkner: *Go Down, Moses* and *Big Woods'*
Faulkner: *The Sound and the Fury*
Gaskell, *Mary Barton*
Hardy: *Tess of the Durbervilles*
Ibsen: *The Doll's House*
Hopkins: Selected Poems
Ted Hughes: *New Selected Poems*
Philip Larkin: *Selected Poems*
Lawrence: Selected Short Stories
Lawrence: *Sons and Lovers*
Lawrence: *Women in Love*
Paul Scott: *The Raj Quartet*
Shakespeare: *Hamlet*

Shakespeare: *Henry IV*
Shakespeare: *King Lear*
Shakespeare: *Richard II*
Shakespeare: *Richard III*
Shakespeare: *The Merchant of Venice*
Shakespeare: *The Tempest*
Shakespeare: *Troilus and Cressida*
Shelley: *Frankenstein*
Wordsworth: *Lyrical Ballads*
Fields of Agony: English Poetry and the First World War

## Philosophy Insights

American Pragmatism
Barthes
Thinking Ethically about Business
Critical Thinking
Existentialism
Formal Logic
Metaethics
Contemporary Philosophy of Religion
Philosophy of Sport
Plato
Wittgenstein
Žižek

## Some Titles in Preparation

Aesthetics
Philosophy of Language
Philosophy of Mind
Political Psychology
Plato's *Republic*
Renaissance Philosophy
Rousseau's legacy

Austen: *Pride and Prejudice*
Blake: *Songs of Innocence & Experience*
Chatwin: *In Patagonia*
Dreiser: *Sister Carrie*
Eliot, George: *Silas Marner*
Eliot: *Four Quartets*
Fitzgerald: *The Great Gatsby*
Hardy: Selected Poems
Heaney: Selected Poems
James: *The Ambassadors*
Lawrence: *The Rainbow*
Melville: *Moby-Dick*
Melville: Three Novellas
Shakespeare: *Macbeth*
Shakespeare: *Romeo and Juliet*
Shakespeare: *Twelfth Night*